KIM
OH
1

REAL
DANGEROUS
GIRL

EDITIONS
HÉRODIADE

PART ONE

Good things happen to you when you work hard. Especially if you also hold a loaded gun to people's heads.
— Cole's Book of Wisdom

ONE

I DIDN'T start out killing people. I had to get to that point. Kind of a work ethic thing.

But once I decided to do it – it worked out. I mean – not for them. The people who got killed. I mean for me.

I leaned my hands on the sink, in the bathroom of that little apartment, and looked in the mirror. A hundred and a few extra pounds – okay, maybe a 110 when I've been porking out – of Korean-American girl, who would've still been in community college if I hadn't taken all those advanced placement classes. Me and every other kid who wanted – or needed – to get out and start making some money before the entire U.S. economy was lying around us in hot, smoking ruins. The blonde cheerleader types might've had bright futures ahead of them as pole dancers, and then marrying whatever IT guys on whose laps they'd already spent their working shifts. But I was a little too meager in the rack department to have that as a realistic career option. And really, Asian girls who get implants just wind up looking like strange Macy's Thanksgiving Day Parade balloons. Guys who go for that are a minority taste, so to speak. So I'd known at an early age I was going to have to work for a living. And I mean grind it out.

Who knew that killing people would make things so much easier for me? Just goes to show that you really do have to be open to the opportunities life presents you.

3

I had to stop thinking about stuff like that and get to work.

I think a lot. It's probably a bad habit.

In the living room, I grabbed my backpack from the couch. The fully loaded, ready-to-go .357 made it heavy. I slung it over my shoulder and headed out the front door.

I had a job to do.

TWO

THE GREAT thing about getting mad – really mad – is that you just don't care what happens. As long as something really bad happens, you're cool with it.

That was something else I had to learn.

† † †

At the beginning, I didn't like Cole. In fact, I hated his guts. Which is funny, when you find out how important he became to me.

Picture this. A canary-yellow '57 Chevy Bel Air convertible cruising down some dark city street . . .

Can you believe that? The nerve that guy had! Of course, that was back when Cole was in his prime, on top of his game and all, but still. Here's a guy who makes his living, essentially, by killing people – and yes, he taught me everything I know – and you'd think the last thing somebody like that would want would be to draw attention to himself. And there he is, cruising along in that dream machine, one hand on top of the steering wheel, the other draped on top of the empty passenger seat beside him. Like he hasn't got a care in the world, or at least none that he couldn't take care of with the big ugly .357 – black, not shiny steel like the one he gave me – he had tucked inside the glove compartment. He could've been Pamela Anderson stark naked on a tricycle, and his ride wouldn't have gotten more long stares from guys than that Bel Air did.

"Dig it," Cole told me once. This was later on, when he had been teaching me stuff. "They see the car. They don't see me. That's the trick. Police come along and ask around, did you see somebody in a yellow '57 Chevy, they're gonna tell the cops all about the car, not me. Like I was the freakin' Invisible Hit Man driving it."

Anyway, here's Cole riding along, on his way to work. You figure it: three in the morning, and the kind of guy he is, he's probably not delivering a pizza. You'd be right about that. Streets are empty, the mercury-vapor lamps overhead are dropping pools of that weird orangey light on the asphalt, the Bel Air's cruising easily along, slowing for a stoplight . . .

He's got the music on. He'd found a custom shop that'd managed to cram a Blaupunkt into the dashboard, just so he could listen to all that dopey metal stuff he likes so much. I never got into that, no matter how long I hung out with him. I'm not exactly the target audience for it.

But that's okay. When you get your lessons in killing people from somebody even a few years older, you have to expect at least a couple creative differences. So to speak.

So Cole's got the Bel Air stopped at the traffic light. That late at night, there's no traffic on the city streets, at least not downtown where the big corporate office towers are. He could just as well slide right through the red light, keep on going to the job he's got lined up. But he doesn't.

"Here's the deal," Cole told me once. "You can break the big rules all you want. Where people like us get messed up is when they break the little ones. Be cool."

Which was true enough in this case, on this night. Because there actually was a patrol car, a regulation black-and-white, parked around the corner. Two cops inside, loafing through their shift, one of them asleep, head tilted back and mouth open. Cole just hadn't spotted it yet.

This is his idea of being cool. Stuck waiting for the light to change, sitting in a convertible where anybody could see what he's doing – so what does he do? He pulls the piece out of the glove compartment, along with a box of the hollow points he preferred, flips the gun chamber open, and starts loading it up. Nodding along to whatever hair band's blaring out of the car stereo . . .

Of course he had given me his big lopsided grin when he had told me all this. He knew what a jerk he was. Proud of it, actually.

He's got the open .357 and the box of ammo in his lap – and that's when the black-and-white creeps forward, from where the cops – or at least the one who'd been awake – had been watching him. Which they would've been doing even if he hadn't been sitting there in a canary yellow '57 Bel Air. The cop behind the steering wheel had been a woman; Cole had looked up and seen her, on a diagonal across the empty intersection. She'd jabbed an elbow into her partner's ribs, waking him up, all blinking and yawning. Then the two of them had sat there, peering at Cole and whatever he was doing in his own car.

"They were lucky," he told me, "that I was already running late. Otherwise things might have gotten less than cool."

So all he'd done was slide the gun and the bullets off his lap, onto the passenger seat beside him. Easy, nothing to hide. While he made eye contact with the lady cop –

And smiled at her.

That had been all he'd had to do. He knew what he had going on, in that department.

"You gals are all the same." Talking like a big ol' redneck hit man. "Even at that distance, I could see her nostrils flare."

The light finally changes, and he gives the Bel Air some gas, just rolling easy through the intersection. Cole looks up in his rear-view mirror and sees the two cops watching him go – well, the female cop is watching him; her partner's just looking at the yellow dreamboat car. Then the black-and-white pulls out into the intersection, turns, and heads off the other way.

Cole reaches over to the passenger seat and one-hands the gun, sliding the last round into the chamber, then closing it up and putting it away. Not back into the glove compartment this time, but inside his jacket . . .

THREE

I WAS working that night, too. My old job, the one I used to do.

There were a lot of nights I was there at the office, way past midnight. That's the problem with doing the accounts for a business that was a little on the funky side, to say the least. It's a lot more work. You're keeping two sets of books, two sets of numbers – one to show the regulators and anybody else who might come snooping around, the other so the boss and his pals could see how much money they were actually making. Like I said, a lot of work.

Not that I minded. I was a total little grind back then. I mean, I'm not exactly glammed up now – I can spend way more money at the gun shop than I'd ever be able to spend at the Nordstrom makeup counter – but then I was even more of a lost cause, sexiness-wise. If it hadn't been for the long black ponytail hanging down the middle of my back, you might've figured I was some Korean-American accountant guy behind my big round glasses, inside my white polyester short-sleeve shirt with the sweat stains under the arms. Amazing how crunching numbers can be so much work – is it any wonder that when I had the chance, I got into killing people instead?

Because if nothing else, I'm stuck behind a computer terminal, with stacks of printouts and receipts and transaction logs all over the desk, in a little

9

windowless office the size of a broom closet – might actually have been one before; it still had that Clorox-and-wet-mold smell – and that putz Cole is out there, having all the fun. It didn't strike me that way back then, because I had my head down in the company accounts all the time, but I think you'd have to admit that there's a basic unfairness in any universe where people – the ones who are working as hard as I was – don't get to ice some jerk every once in a while. Just my opinion, but the American workplace would be a lot happier if a few more worthwhile murders were allowed. I've been there.

Meanwhile, over at some other big tall office building in the city, there's a limo pulling up to the curb in the front. Three in the morning, all kinds of business being taken care of – just not the kind most people get to hear about.

First out of the back seat of the limo are a couple of black-suited bodyguards, crew-cut types shaped like walking refrigerators and just about as smart. But good at their jobs. These two muscle types get out and stand on the sidewalk, scanning the area with each one of them keeping a hand inside his jacket, ready to pull out some ugly cannon if they spot anything funny. Their whole function is to get whoever's inside the limo from one place to another, without their boss getting drilled in a public place. Like right out here on the street. That's an important job, at least as far as their boss might be concerned, and it's totally taking up all the brain cells in their heads. No room for anything else – their hard, slit-eyed gazes are scoping out everything, every building, every street, every alley-like radar dishes turned down level to the horizon.

The only thing they're not catching is Cole, watching them from around a corner a block away. When he wants to, he's spooky good at not being seen. In this movie, he's already left the screaming yellow Bel Air a couple streets away, and gone sneaking the rest of the distance to his target, slipping like a ghost from one dark spot to another. Until he's right on top of them . . .

All clear, at least as far as the bodyguards can tell. One keeps watch, constantly scanning, hand inside his jacket, while the other turns back to the limo. He reaches into the limo and helps out the figure who's been patiently sitting there on the rear seat, waiting for his crew to make sure everything's safe. A smaller man, silver-haired, groomed with that sleek gloss that rich and powerful people just naturally acquire along the way – he steps out of the limo and walks without hurry, flanked by the taller, wider bulk of the two bodyguards, toward the glass front door of the building.

I know all this, and can see it, because Cole told me all about it. Telling me about his own jobs, the ones he pulled off for the creep we'd both been working for back then – that was all part of my education.

At the office tower door, one of the bodyguards takes his gun out of his jacket and uses the butt of it to rap against the glass. A uniformed security guard comes scurrying out from behind his station in the building's lobby, unlocks the door, and lets the trio in. The guard oozes all sorts of cringing respect to the white-haired one in the middle, tugging at the bill of his uniform cap, nodding and smiling in the nervous way flunkies get when they're confronted by somebody this big and powerful. None of this makes any impact, of course, on the boss – he's been getting that response, or something like it, most of his life. It's like the weather to him; there, but not worth noticing.

From his nice and hidden vantage point, Cole watches the important boss guy get shepherded safely into the building. He can see one of the guards staying with the smaller man as the security guards relock the building's front door. The other bodyguard goes back out to the limo, leans into the rolled-down window up front and says something to the driver, then leans back against the side of the limo, keeping watch, arms folded across his chest.

That's all fine as far as Cole is concerned. It's not like he was going to try anything stupid right out there in the open. That's not his style. And it's not what he taught me. Which is why I'm alive, and some other people aren't.

Instead, Cole pulls back from the corner of the building where he had been hanging out and walks down to where he had left the duffel bag that he had taken out of the Bel Air's trunk, when he had parked it streets away. The big green Army-style duffel is heavy enough – it's got his tools in it, the stuff he uses to do his job – that it takes an effort to get its wide canvas strap slung over his shoulder. Cole's got some pretty good muscle tone – at least he did back then, before all the bad things happened to him. More than I'll ever have, that's for sure – but it's not like he's some sort of hypertrophied weight lifter.

"Just enough to get the job done." Another thing he told me when he'd been schooling me in the fine points of my new career. "Anything more just gets in the way."

Cole has got his tool bag slung over his shoulder. He turns and keeps on walking away from that other office tower he had been watching. He's got another route already set up, to get to where he needs to be.

Which is one of the city's older office buildings, the kind that have some sort of historical registry brass plaque on the front, and the offices inside are all shabby and disreputable, full of insurance agents with no clients and Chinese dentists with pre-World War II equipment. You know the kind of place, somewhere somebody like you wouldn't go into in a million years –

Cole wasn't going into it, either. Instead, he goes around to the dirty, garbage-strewn alley in the back. A couple of slinky stray cats watch him as he pulls down the fire escape's rusty ladder. With the duffel bag slung on his back, he starts climbing up.

In the meantime, while Cole's doing all sorts of fun, neat stuff out in the night, I'm still stuck at my desk, grinding away at the numbers.

"Okay," I mumble as I paw through a sheaf of accounts receivable. "It's gotta be here somewhere . . ." When I'd get tired, I used to talk to myself. Maybe just to keep myself company. A lot of times, working that late, I figured I was the only one there, except maybe for the janitors mopping the floors.

Turns out, this time I wasn't.

But back to Cole. His movie's a lot more interesting than mine was, at least back then.

He gets to the top of the old office building and throws his duffel bag onto the roof. It lands there with a clanking thud that echoes away in the night. But nobody hears it except him. He boosts himself from the top platform of the fire escape and scrambles onto the roof. He picks up the duffel bag by its strap and heads toward the other side. When he reaches the roof's edge, he stops and takes a look around.

What Cole sees is another old building next to this one, separated by a dark gap. Beyond that is the back side of the much bigger and taller, all sleek and silvery-glassy, office tower that he had been watching before.

Cole lowers the duffel bag, bends over it, and opens it up. From inside the bag, he takes out a coil of rope, glistening high-tech mountain-climber stuff, that he paid a lot of money for. He always paid top dollar for his equipment – but then again, just like a mountain climber, his life pretty much depended on it. That, and getting the job done, whatever it was.

Knotted on one end of the rope was a big grappling hook, the sort of thing you only see in movies like this one, where people are doing this sort of cool thing. You can't buy something like that at Walmart, at least not in most towns. Cole told me he bought the three-pronged hook at some maritime salvage dump, out by the wharves. It wasn't so expensive, just hard to find.

From where he was standing, he could see the next building's fire escape. He gave the rope some length, swinging the grappling hook at its end in a slow vertical circle, just brushing the roof. Then he leaned forward and let the hook go, sailing across the gap between the two buildings. First try, the hook catches, one of its prongs snagging on the rusting metal of the other building's fire escape. Easy enough for him – he'd done this before.

That other fire escape was a few feet lower than the roof of the office building he was standing on. So no problem looping the duffel bag onto the rope and letting it slide across the gap. With a little tugging and lifting, the duffel was safely deposited on the flat bars of the other building's fire escape. Another sharper tug and the loop securing the duffel bag to the rope came undone. That left Cole with an unencumbered line hooked to the opposite building.

Which was all he needed to do one of his circus tricks, the sort of thing he did to get his jobs done. Putting a foot on the rope to keep it from slipping away, he pulled out of his jacket pocket a pair of heavy leather gloves, the thick palms polished shiny from use, and tugged them on. He pulled the rope taut, looping it around his gloved hands, and clenched his fists tight. He stepped onto the roof's raised edge, jumped off, and swung Tarzan-like across the gap.

Sort of, at least. Because the rope's anchor point on the opposite fire escape was lower than the roof he was starting from, first there was a drop of several yards. He had to hunch himself up and brace himself for the impact, to keep his arms from being pulled out of their sockets. And at the same time, bend his knees and cock his legs so that the nubbed soles of his Red Wing workingman's boots came flat against the other building's outside wall.

If there had been some wino who had woken up in the shelter of one of the dumpsters in the alley below, he would've witnessed some pretty impressive aerial action happening above him. And maybe there had been; it wouldn't have mattered to Cole, as he went about his business.

Like I said, he'd done this sort of thing before. On other jobs. A couple of seconds of rope action later, pulling himself hand-over-hand, and then he was scrabbling onto the fire escape just below the one he had landed his duffel bag on. He climbed the rusty metal ladder, grabbed the duffel, and continued on up to the other building's roof.

FOUR

TURNS OUT I wasn't the only one there, that late in the office.

Close in on Little Nerd Accountant Girl – I was hardly more than a teenager then, though just barely – sweating away in her cheap white polyester shirt, dripping sweat from her brow onto the reports spread out on the desk in front of her. There was $73 missing somewhere, and by God, I was going to find it.

"Aha!" Little Nerd Accountant Girl's eyes light up behind her big round glasses. A misplaced decimal point, a number that had looked like a nine the first time around, but now she realized it was a five – something real exciting like that. She bends her head over the printouts, scribbling on them with a pencil. "Now we're getting somewhere . . ."

She looks up blinking, mouth open like a moron, when there's a knock on the door.

Back to Cole's part of the movie. That is much more interesting.

Now he's standing on the roof of the second office building, at its edge with the duffel bag beside him, looking over at the bigger office tower. There's a window-washing platform way up at the top, slung over the side by a pair of gantry arms. That's how the office tower stays so nice and shiny, gleaming in the moonlight like sculptured ice. Nobody's washing any windows now, though. Which means that the platform is just sitting up there, ready for Cole to use it.

He takes from the duffel bag a little electronic device with buttons and a numbered dial on its surface. The thing looks a little crude and home-made – it should, since Cole built it himself, doing all the soldering on the circuit board inside and then wrapping the thing up in black electrician's tape. He's good on the technical details, but the aesthetics part has always been a little beyond him.

"If it works," he told me once, "that's all I care. The rest of the world should operate on that basis."

Close up on the device in Cole's hand as he pushes some of the buttons on it. He looks over at the window-washing platform at the top of the office tower. Nothing's happened; it's still just sitting there. He makes some adjustments with the dial on the device and pushes the buttons again. Success. The motors hooked up to the gantry cables come to life. The window-washing platform starts lowering itself slowly down the side of the office tower.

During the day, of course, the sound of the gantry motors would've been swallowed up, lost in the sounds of traffic from the street below, all the various noises of the city going on around the place. In the middle of the night, past three in the morning, you can hear them.

The bodyguard leaning against the limo, out in front of the office tower, certainly hears the motor noise. He looks upward, scowling, trying to locate where the sound's coming from. In his line of work, anything unusual happening is not good.

On the roof of the old office building, Cole takes out from the duffel another piece of his neat-o working gear. It's a collapsible metal ladder, for which he also paid a lot of money. The high-tech alloy it's made out of is light enough for him to carry, but strong enough to bear his weight when he has it unfolded all the way. He watches the window-washing platform coming down the side of the office tower for another couple of seconds, then pushes another button on his little home-made black box. The gantry motors stop, their cables vibrating like giant violin strings for a moment, leaving the platform directly opposite from where he's planted himself. He picks up the extended metal ladder from the office building roof and swings it in a horizontal arc across the gap. The collapsible ladder is just long enough – he knew it would be – to reach from the edge of the office building roof over to the tower's window-washing platform. The L-shaped hooks at the end of the ladder catch onto the platform rail.

That gives Cole a narrow passage right over to the office tower. Of course, he doesn't walk across like a tightrope artist – he's not crazy, at least not in that way. He crawls across the horizontal ladder on his hands and knees, going from one rung to the next.

Granted, that's still not the kind of thing you or I might want to do. I mean, picture it: yeah, the collapsible ladder's all high-tech and stuff, some alloy they build the Space Shuttle out of, or something like that, but it's still bending under Cole's weight, each careful forward shifting of his weight causing it to bounce up and down a little. I would've been puking from sheer dizzying fear by the time I was halfway across – too bad for the wino down in the alley, looking up at me – and then I would've frozen witless, hands locked on one of the ladder rungs, the only thought in my head being a serious reconsideration of my life choices so far . . .

Cole, on the other hand, dug this sort of stuff. So maybe he really was crazy back then.

He inches across the ladder, with the duffel bag tightened onto his back. Then close up on him as he finally reaches the other side and scrambles onto the window-washing platform. He stands up, takes a deep breath – and hears the collapsible ladder making a different, kind of creaking noise behind him.

"Damn –" He looks over his shoulder and sees the ladder tilting and swaying. Over on the other side of the gap, the edge of the old building's roof has started to crumble away. Then it gives way completely, the other end of the ladder swinging down toward the outside of the big office tower. Cole has just enough time to dive for the end of the ladder that's hooked onto the rail of the window-washing platform he's standing on. He holds onto the ladder, bracing himself as the loose end clangs against the tower below him.

That was way more noise than he had been planning on making. The impact's clang bounces, echoing off the flanks of every building for blocks around, then dies away. He lifts his head and listens, trying to catch any other sound in the night.

Of course, if the ladder bridge had given way while he had been halfway across, he would've been dead.

Stuff like that never bothered him. The only thing on his mind was knowing that the bodyguard stationed by the limo might be shouting into his cell phone right now, alerting his partner inside that there was something funky going on, while he ran with his gun raised up in his other hand, heading around the corner of the tower and toward where all the noise had come from.

A couple of seconds tick by, with nothing like that happening. Cole relaxes a bit, then hauls the ladder up onto the platform, collapses it back down, and stows it away again inside the duffel bag. He looks around the platform and finds its set of controls, mounted on the rail. He pushes a green button, and the gantry motors come to life again, hauling the platform up toward the top of the tower . . .

Back in my part of the movie, the Little Nerd Accountant Girl is watching the door of her office. She's such a timid little mouse – hard to believe, but I really was back then – she probably figures it's somebody who sneaked into the building, come to murder her. Or some other fate worse than death, if whoever it was had been able to figure out that I actually was a girl, with the appropriate equipment somewhere under those dorky knee-length plaid skirts I used to wear.

That was the sort of crap I used to worry about. Things are a little different now. To put it mildly.

Meanwhile, Cole was having still more fun.

FIVE

COLE'S ON the roof, and nobody seems to know, even with the screwup of the collapsible ladder nearly falling down to the alley below. He crosses over to the other side of the tower's roof, the side overlooking the street, and checks. Way down there, the one bodyguard is still leaning back against the side of the limo, arms folded across his chest. Everything under control. Which suited Cole fine.

"When you're out making trouble for people –" More words of wisdom from my instructor. "You want them believing for as long as possible that God loves them, and they got nothing to worry about."

If they'd been able to see Cole and what he was doing, they would've worried, all right. Because now he was really getting down to work.

From the duffel bag, he takes out another electronic device, one he didn't build himself. Something called a Camero Xaver 400, made by some company in Israel. That one was seriously expensive. In real movies, you see SWAT teams and secret agents using thermal imaging devices to see through walls and inside buildings. Those actually don't work, at least not the way they do in the special effects shots. The Xaver 400 does – it's got some kind of high-tech, Ultra-Wideband radar going on. Cole switches on the device, sets it flat on the tower roof, and peers at the lit-up screen. And at whatever might be going on down below.

21

Which right at the moment was the private executive elevator bringing the white-haired guy and the other bodyguard up to the top level. In the plush mahogany-paneled reception area on that floor, the numbers light up above the elevator doors. They open, and the white-haired guy steps out. There are people waiting for him, including another important-looking dude, this one broader across the shoulders and with thinning salt-and-pepper hair. He's flanked by his own pair of bodyguards. Gives a big smile to his partner who's just arrived, and a wave of the lit Cohiba in one hand; the cigar's thick around as a baby's arm. The white-haired guy turns and gives some instructions to his bodyguard, who stations himself by the elevator doors. With a thump across the first one's shoulders, the other important guy ushers him into the conference room past the reception area, the two bulky bodyguards following them inside.

Up on the office tower roof, Cole has had mixed luck with the Xaver 400. Good as it is, there are too many pipes and ducts and other stuff running right under his feet, to get any kind of clear picture about who might be moving around inside. But that's all right; he always has a backup plan. He throws the Xaver 400 into the duffel bag and takes out another gizmo, this one with what looks like a doctor's stethoscope headset attached to it. Basically a high-sensitivity microphone-in-a-box – he puts on the headset, cranks up the device's amplifier, and starts moving the sensor around in a widening spiral, kneeling down and moving from spot to spot on the roof.

Bingo. He can hear voices down there. Not clearly enough to make out what anyone's saying, but definite enough to know exactly where they are. Which is all he needs at the moment. He pulls off the headset and throws the gear back in the duffel. Now the real fun will start . . .

Right about that time, Little Accountant Nerd Girl is all relieved to see that it's just her boss standing in the doorway of her crummy cubbyhole office, and not some mad murderer who'd somehow gotten into the building after-hours.

"How's it going?" A big smile from him.

Actually, knowing what I do now about the guy, I should've preferred the murderer I'd been imagining in my scared little mind.

"It's . . . it's going fine, Mr. McIntyre." I sit back with my hands in my lap. "Just fine."

"No, it's not. Otherwise you still wouldn't be here this late."

He liked to come across all kind of concerned. Like he was the good kind of boss. I was still fooled by him back then.

"Well . . ." Now I was embarrassed, because I knew how ratty and sweaty I must've looked. "It's been better. There are a couple of the club accounts that are off."

"By how much?"

"Um . . ." In my throat, my voice dwindles down to a timid little squeak. Like it's my fault. "A couple thousand, actually."

He keeps on smiling. He's got a Hermès tie on, the knot loosened, and a nicely tailored suit that's worth more than everything I own.

"You're worried about that?"

I can't answer. Can't even breathe. He can't see it, but I'm wringing my hands into bloodless knots underneath the desk. I can't even look at him.

"Kim," he says, all kindly and paternal and stuff. "What does a few thousand matter? Really."

"It does matter, Mr. McIntyre." A mouse could've spoken up louder. I'm still staring down at the reports scattered across the desk. They're going all blurry, as though my glasses were filling up with salt water. "Things like that . . . they add up after a while."

"I knew you'd say that. Look. Here's what I want you to do, Kim. Give it your best shot for another, oh, I don't know – maybe another quarter-hour. All right? And if you don't crack it, you don't find the money, then don't worry about it. Just go on home. Try again tomorrow, when you're fresh. Okay? I'm serious."

Little Accountant Nerd Girl bites her lip and manages to nod, still looking down at the papers and all the blurry numbers. I would've died for the man right about then. That's what kind of twit I was.

"All right, Mr. McIntyre." Nothing but a whisper. "I will."

"Promise?"

I nodded again.

"And give Donnie a hug for me when you finally get home."

Another nod, and even a brave little smile, to myself.

Just as I'm aware of him stepping back out into the hallway and pulling my office door shut, he stops and says something else. "Oh – one more thing, Kim –"

This time I manage to look up at him.

"Actually, I'm kind of glad you're still here. And if you could stay just a little longer, that'd be great."

The smile fades. Because I already know what he's going to say.

"Cole might swing by later. So if you could have a check ready for him . . ."

I don't move, but there's already a lump of ice in my gut. My spine's gone completely rigid, as though somebody just shoved a poker up my schoolgirl butt.

"Sure." I nodded. This was the part of my job I hated the most. Having to deal with Cole. "I'll take care of it." I knew what account my boss wanted the payment to come from. The one that was way off the books. "You don't have to worry about anything."

"I knew I could count on you."

"Great." His big nice-boss smile again. "Good night."

I just sat there trembling, even after the door was shut. I didn't say anything until I could hear the elevator at the end of the hallway, heading down to the building's lobby.

"Shit!"

Little Nerd Accountant Girl was in a bad mood. That was just about as scary as I got back then.

How times change.

I went back to work, and I found the missing receipts. They'd gotten stuck on the back of one of the plastic binders. That cleared up all my problems for the time being.

Except for that jerk Cole.

SIX

COLE'S ON the office tower roof. And he can hear the elevator coming up. The structure housing the motors and the cables is right up there on the roof with him. At its door, he runs through his set of passkeys until he finds one that works. Inside, the sound of the big motors and the thick, braided cables running over the machinery's reels is louder. Then it's all suddenly quieter when he goes over to the control panel and flips the emergency power cut-off switch. The reels and the cables grind to a halt.

He has a good idea of what's going on down below him, on the top floor of the office tower. The red numbers above the elevator doors blink off. The bodyguard standing there notices, looking up over his shoulder at the dead numbers. He instinctively reaches inside his jacket, grabbing his holstered gun. Anything unusual is not good.

Cole keeps on working. He needs to reduce some other numbers, namely the amount of people he needs to deal with so he can complete the job. He's already got his ugly black .357 raised in one hand as he looks over the front edge of the building, down toward where the limo is parked at the curb.

The bodyguard who had been left stationed down there has relaxed enough to light up a cigarette, while he's talking with the limo driver sticking his head out the passenger side window.

It's a clear shot for Cole, straight down. He wraps both hands around the butt of the gun and fires. The bullet goes right through the top of the bodyguard's head, dropping him onto his chest, arms splayed out. The lit cigarette rolls down the sidewalk, scattering sparks.

For a moment, the limo driver gapes stunned at the body lying where his buddy had been standing and talking to him just a second before. In the diminished spectrum from the streetlights, the pool of blood widening below the bodyguard's head looks black as ink. Stupidly, the limo driver lifts his wide-eyed gaze up toward where the shot had come from. The second bullet from Cole's .357 catches him right in the face, leaving his corpse hanging out the limo window.

The bodyguard inside had to have heard the shots, Cole figured, given that they had come from the building roof just above him. He's already got his own gun out in one hand, and is shouting into his cell phone in his other, trying to get some answer from the guard out on the street about what's going on. There's no answer.

Cole's not hanging around, waiting. He's working. He's tucked the .357 back into his jacket, and he's pulling the next thing he needs out of the duffel bag. It looks like a brick, only shiny black and with a digital kitchen timer duct-taped to the top. It's actually a big chunk of something called RDX, which stands for Research Department Explosive, mixed with some plasticizers and a few special ingredients that Cole came up with on his own. A chemist would know the stuff ascyclotrimethylene trinitramine. He'd also know that it's bad news for anybody unfortunate enough to be standing close to it when it goes off. Cole sets the brick down right where his fancy electronic gear had indicated there were people below. He hits the start button on the timer, grabs the duffel bag by its strap, and sprints for the far edge of the office tower roof. There's just enough seconds for him to dive over the edge and land on his shoulder on the window-washing platform hanging there –

Even with the shaped-charge housing he'd stuffed the RDX into, there's still an impressive explosion that comes roaring up from the roof of the office tower. Across town, in another building, Little Nerd Accountant Girl looks up from her number-crunching, wondering what that funny whoof! sound is, coming from the distance. If the cubbyhole where her boss had shunted her had had a window, she might've been able to see the big orange fireball rolling up into the night sky, like the special effects in some Die Hard-type action flick, instead of the sad little soap opera I was starring in back then.

Most of the explosive's force goes straight down into the office tower, though, the way Cole had planned it. He's tucked down safe on the window-washing platform below the roof edge, covering his ears as the fiery wash rolls out above him. It only lasts a couple of seconds. Taking his hands from his ears, he can hear chunks of debris raining back down on the rooftop. Soon as that noise dwindles down to the last few bits thrown up into the air by the blast, he's pulled himself back up onto the roof and is running toward the gaping hole, ragged and burnt, that the RDX had ripped open. He's got his gun in hand again, carrying it straight up with its barrel held out away from his head.

There's all kinds of chaos down on the top floor of the office tower. Which is just what Cole wants to be going on there. The bodyguard by the elevator doors has been knocked flat by the explosion, hard enough to crush his nose and break his cheekbone against polished tiles. Peering through the smoke rising up from the hole, gun aimed downward now, Cole is just able to see the guard staggering up onto his feet. One quick shot catches the bodyguard in the back of the head, dropping him onto his knees for a moment, before the corpse sprawls on its bloodied face.

More shouting, coming through the banks of smoke beginning to fill up the space. From out of the conference burst the two remaining bodyguards, guns drawn, scanning across the mess in front of them, looking for whoever's coming in through the broken roof –

Which won't be Cole. He had a whole theory of operations, which he passed on to me. It included the principle that in his line of business – and mine now – you never want to be where people are expecting you to be. So the bodyguards are coughing and fighting their way through the smoke left from the blast, waving their guns around, trying to catch a bead on whoever just fired and took out their buddy by the elevators –

And Cole has already sprinted back across the roof, away from the plume of black, ashy smoke churning up into the night sky. He's jumped over the edge of the roof again, back down onto the window-washing platform. He picks up the duffel bag's shoulder strap in both hands and uses the bag, heavy from all the equipment inside it, as a battering ram against the window glass that the platform is hanging next to. With the second swinging blow, the window shatters, the razor-sharp pieces raining down the side of the building. Cole lifts the bag high enough to brush away any shards that are left hanging at the top of the window frame, then drops the bag on the platform, climbs over its rail, and leaps into the building.

This is the real action part.

Cole has his gun out again, and he's running down the office tower corridor, toward the smoke and the shouting. The bodyguards don't see him coming. They're too fixated on where he used to be, up on the office tower roof.

One of them comes to his senses and remembers his real job, taking care of their bosses. The bodyguard runs back to the conference room, grabs the arms of both the important-looking men, the white-haired one and the larger one, and steers them across the shattered, burning reception area. He slams his palm against the elevator button. Nothing happens. He looks up and can see through the smoke that the little red numbers aren't lighting up above the elevator doors. It's dead, no way out using it –

"Come on!" The bodyguard grabs the two bosses and pulls them toward the door. "Let's move it –" They follow his commands without protest. He's the professional, the one in charge now, the one who'll get them out alive.

There's an emergency door at the end of the corridor, with the green EXIT sign just barely visible through the smoke filling up the space. It'll be a long stumbling run down all the floors to the ground level, but that's the only way out now.

Or it would have been if Cole hadn't already gotten there. The two bosses are stunned by the sharp crack of the gunshot echoing through the corridor. From between the two of them, the bodyguard is lifted off his feet by the bullet slamming into his chest and thrown backward. He's dead, his chest blossoming red in the smoke-dimmed light, by the time he lands on the floor.

The white-haired important-looking man is still staring down at the corpse, then turns and looks into the muzzle of the .357 that Cole is holding straight-armed into the boss's face. That's the last thing he sees, as Cole pulls the trigger.

Now there are two corpses on the corridor's floor, one of them drilled right between the eyes. The other important-looking guy, the taller one, backs up against the wall, his own wide-eyed gaze locked on the gun in Cole's hand.

"Don't worry –" Cole shakes his head. "You're not on my list. Not tonight, at least."

The last of the bodyguards stumbles into the corridor. Cole snaps the .357 up, aiming it straight at this one.

"Hey, don't – it's cool, man –" The bodyguard tosses away his gun and holds his hands up in the air. "You don't have to take me out. I'm good –"

Cole lowers the .357 and watches as the guard comes over and looks at the dead bodies.

"Damn." The bodyguard looks up at him. "Why'd you have to step into my shit like this? Do this on my watch and all. You and me used to work together. Remember? These kinds of gigs are hard to get."

"So?" Cole shrugs. "They might keep you on."

"After this? I doubt it."

"You got that right." The taller, salt-and-pepper-haired man has regained some of his boss-like attitude. He might still be rattled from seeing his white-haired buddy popped right in front of him, but not so much that he can't ream somebody else out. "What the hell good are you? You're fired."

"See?" The bodyguard scowls at Cole. "Told you."

"Not my problem." Cole waves the thickening smoke away from his face. Flames are starting to flicker out of the reception area door. "See you around."

"You just going to leave us here?' The ex-bodyguard shouts after him. "That's cold, man."

"Don't worry –" Cole doesn't even look back over his shoulder as he leaves. "Fire Department's on its way."

He's right about that. On the soundtrack of this movie, the sirens can be heard wailing in the distance, getting closer and louder.

The window-washing platform's as good as an elevator. Cole climbs back out the window he shattered and over the platform rail. He hits the control button and rides the platform all the way down to the surface level. The fire trucks' red lights are swooping across the front of the building as he picks up his duffel bag, slings it over his shoulder, and walks casually, no hurry, back toward where he left the Bel Air . . .

† † †

I'm still working away on the company accounts. I mean that person I used to be.

Little Nerd Accountant Girl is startled to look up and see Cole standing in the doorway of her tiny, cramped office. He's done that before; he loves to do the spooky thing of just showing up, sneaking in to places without making any sound to give him away. And he's good at that sort of thing – it comes with his line of work.

"Got a check for me?"

She stares at him, her breath caught in her throat, her heart speeding up. She's so scared, she's about ready to wet herself. He's got that psychotic lopsided smile, and he smells of fire and explosives and general craziness. There's something spattered across his shirt and his jacket that she's pretty sure is blood. He's every kind of bad news in the world, just leaning against the side of the doorway and watching her, all easy and stuff. The only thing is that she loathes him so – or at least I used to – that she doesn't want to give him the satisfaction that would come with showing how scared she was. At least I had that much guts back then.

"Sure." She keeps control of herself as she pulls open one of the desk drawers and takes out the check ledger. The check's already made out – not to Cole personally, but to something called CNS Courier Services, which was just the bogus company he used as a front. She hadn't wanted to write all that out with him standing there, because she knew she wouldn't have been able to keep her hand from trembling and messing it up. She pulls the check from the ledger and holds it out. "Here you go."

Cole takes the check and looks it over. Even though he doesn't need to – it's always for the same amount, no matter the size of the job. It's a lot, especially by the accountant's standards. More than she makes in a year. But that's what McIntyre pays the guy, for services rendered.

He points to the ledger on the desk in front of her. "You can put down that this is for the Winterhalter job." He slides the check inside his jacket. "You can tell your boss that he probably won't need a follow-up on this one."

She doesn't know everything about her boss's business – except what's there in the numbers – but she knows that name. One of McIntyre's competitors, who had been planning on joining forces with another guy like him. If Cole said that the job had been taken care of, though, it meant that hook-up wasn't going to happen anytime soon.

She still glares at him. "You know," she says, "I had to wait here to pay you." The clock on the wall shows it's now past four in the morning. "I've got a life, too."

"I'm sure you do." There were plenty of women who would have found his smile charming. She didn't. "My apologies."

When he was gone, she sat there fuming, scowling at the space in the doorway where he'd been. Not mad at him, not anymore, but at herself . . .

Cole heads back to his place. Where he lives, sort of, but mainly where he keeps all the stuff that he uses to do his job.

Later on, he told me all about it. About what would be waiting for him back then, when he'd get back from work. So to speak.

The place is over in the city's shipping district, out by the wharves. You wouldn't expect somebody like Cole to live in a normal sort of place.

He leaves the yellow Bel Air out in front of one of the warehouses – everybody around there knows better than to touch it – and unlocks a little office-type door beside one of the freight docks. Nothing much going on at that hour, except a big container vessel from Japan being off-loaded at the farthest wharf, the big one with the cranes that can pluck whole boxcars out of a ship's hold. He doesn't pay it any attention; that's just the kind of business that goes on around here. Plus his business. Like his car, people know better than to poke their noses into that.

His girlfriend Monica is sleeping on a mattress on the warehouse floor, a blanket pulled over herself and a half-empty wine bottle a couple feet away. She's good-looking, in that armor-plated, avaricious way that a guy like him would be attracted to. Three guesses what she worked at, and you'd be right on the first one.

Cole looks at her for a moment, sleeping there, then takes off his jacket and throws it over to one side, followed by his shirt. They both wind up draped over an automatic rifle leaned against the wall. The place is total gun-nut hell, just full of that kind of thing, and worse. The kind of stuff that Cole uses to do his job. Plus a workbench scattered with tools, a welding tank and torch, some smaller electronics assembly gear – like I already told you, to do the kind of things he does, he needs to build some of the gear.

Standing there bare-chested, Cole nudges his girlfriend's shoulder with the toe of his boot. With her eyes still closed, she groggily mutters something about what he can go do with himself. "Leave me alone, will ya?"

He pokes her again, a little harder. This time, he manages to get her to sit up, holding the blanket up against her breasts. Her long red hair is all tangled and sexy-looking, if that's the kind of think you like. For Cole, it is.

Monica knows it, too. She's awake enough now to smile at him. "How'd it go?"

"Fine." He doesn't need to fill in the details. They've been together for a while. "Piece of cake."

"I bet." She fumbles around the mattress, looking for her cigarettes.

"Got something for you."

She glances back over at him and sees that he's undone his belt, the one with the big enameled Confederate flag emblem for a buckle that he likes to wear, to let people know just how politically incorrect he is. As if that were ever in doubt.

"So I can see." She leans forward, unzips his fly, and spreads the front of his trousers. Not what you're thinking; this is a different sort of movie.

What she sees there is the check I'd cut for him a little while ago, back at my office. He's got it tucked in the waistband of his boxer shorts, poking out so the number on it can be read.

Monica doesn't say anything more. She just leans even farther forward, bites the top of the check, and pulls it out with her teeth. She's smiling as she looks up at him.

That's just the kind of relationship they had.

A little while later, they're both lying on the mattress; she's got her head lying on his chest, and is slowly regaining her breath. The check's somewhere on the warehouse floor, where it had gotten tossed. The wine bottle's empty now, except for the couple of cigarette butts at the bottom.

"Nothing's ever gonna change, baby." Cole drowsily murmurs, as he runs his hand through her hair. He wasn't exhausted before, even after all his running and jumping around over at that big office tower – but he is now. "That's the best part." He slowly nods, eyes closed. "Nothing's ever gonna change . . ."

Just goes to show. Even somebody smart as him. The world's always capable of taking you by surprise.

SEVEN

GOOD THING for me that the cross-town express bus ran twenty-four hours. The bad thing was that I still had to walk about a dozen creepy, badly lit blocks to get from the bus stop to my apartment building. That late, I didn't feel safe until I got the front door unlocked, then slammed shut behind me.

Mr. McIntyre had told me to give Donnie a hug for him, when I got home. So I did that, sitting on the edge of his bed. He'd waited up for me.

Donnie's my younger brother. All the family I have.

"You were there a long time." He said it with an accusatory tone of voice. Not accusing me, but the whole big world that wasn't as nice to me as he thought it should be. "It's practically morning."

"It is morning, honey." I sat there with my shoulders slumped, feeling all worn and weary. "Any time after midnight, it's morning. Technically."

"I mean morning as in time for you to get up and go to work. When the sun comes up."

"Yeah . . . I know."

"You should go in late. Your boss won't mind."

"Can't." I was so tired, I couldn't even think. Not just from being there so late, but from having to deal with Cole. Even for just the few minutes it took to give him his check. Somehow, that always took it out of me. "I gotta stick it out," I told Donnie. I put my hand on the chrome arm of his wheelchair and rolled it back and forth a couple of inches. "Just a little while longer. Then things will be different."

He smiled. This was a little routine we had going between us.

"How different?"

I wrapped both my arms around him again, and rocked the both of us. "Real different," I said. "Different as . . ." My tired brain tried to come up something new. But couldn't. "Different as night and day."

"Ducks and oranges."

"You and me." I sat back from him. "From everybody else. That's how different."

It wasn't much of a game. But we'd been doing it for a long time.

"Okay, pal." I stood up from the edge of the bed. "You should've gone to sleep a long time ago. Don't get on my case about this sort of thing."

"Okay." Donnie laid back against his pillow and pulled the covers over himself. The apartment was freezing, but the landlord wouldn't turn the heat on unless there was actually ice forming on the insides of the windows. "I left dinner for you in the fridge. In the green bowl, on the second shelf."

That bugged me a little bit, but I wasn't going to chew him out about it at the moment. When I wasn't there, it was usually too much trouble for him to deal with the wheelchair, so he'd just scoot himself around on the floor. Which meant quite a stretch for him to accomplish anything in the kitchenette area, but he'd somehow manage. I was just afraid he was going to set fire to the whole place someday. How would he get out? And even if he did, it would just be one more piece of bad luck, losing what little stuff we had, right when things were going to finally turn around for us. We didn't need that now.

"I'm not hungry," I told him.

"Yeah, right." He gave me one of his hard glares, which from a kid his age were usually more funny than intimidating. "You gotta keep your strength up, Kimmie."

"I'll have it for breakfast."

"You don't even know what it is."

"Whatever it is." He had a limited range, given what I usually managed to carry in from the store on the corner. Pretty much always something with rice, not because of any ethnic thing going on with us, but just because the stuff was cheap, and that was what we could afford with what I was bringing in from my crappy job. All that was going to change, though, and soon. I leaned over and kissed him on the forehead. "I promise."

That mollified him enough for him to close his eyes and turn his head to one side on the pillow. I switched off the light and closed the door, going out to the front room where I slept. On the sway-backed couch that had come with the place. Sometimes there's an advantage to being short; at least I didn't have to hang my feet over one of the upholstered arms.

Which didn't matter, at least in this part of the movie I'm telling you about. I couldn't sleep. Not just because of getting rattled by having to deal with that jerk Cole – the way I always got when I had to cut him a check – but just because there was too much going on inside my head.

You know how it is when there's a thunderstorm heading your way? Even the air seems to get tense, expectant. Something's going to happen. And I knew that it was. Even if it's something you know is going to be good, your stomach's still doing flip-flops.

So I'm lying there curled up on that broken-down couch, in my pajama shorts and the extra-large man's

T-shirt that I used to put on back then, whenever I was emotional. I still have it, though I don't wear it much anymore. Don't need to, I guess, because I'm so hard and dangerous and all these days. But the T-shirt still means something to me. Not because it belonged to my dad or anything like that – when you're a kid going through the Child Protective Services system, you pretty much lose all that kind of stuff. They probably figure it's better if you don't have anything to remind you of your parents. And maybe they're right. Donnie remembers them better than I do, or at least he says he does. So the T-shirt had actually belonged to one of our foster dads, the one that had been the nicest to us back when CPS had been shuffling the two of us through places out in Middle of Nowhere, Oklahoma. We'd only been with the guy and his wife for less than a year – but I kept the T-shirt, anyway.

Well, it wasn't doing any good this time. You're watching this movie on the screen inside your head, and there's not much happening in it at the moment – nothing fun like people getting killed and stuff, at least – just the Little Nerd Accountant Girl that I was, lying curled up in a ball on a ratty furnished-apartment sofa, staring up at the ceiling. But there's another movie, one that she's been watching for a while now. Nothing much happens in it, but she watches it over and over, just the same.

Here's what happens in that movie going on inside her head. That used to be my head. She's sitting behind her desk in her stuffy little cubbyhole office at work, going over more numbers – it doesn't matter which one. Just any kind of numbers. And she looks up, and there's her boss Mr. McIntyre standing in the office doorway, just the way he had been a little while before. And he gives her that same big nice-boss smile . . .

Kim, he says in that movie inside her head. It's time. Time for some big changes around here. Still smiling. I hope you're ready for them.

"Oh, yes –" The girl curled up on the couch squeezes her eyes shut and whispers the words aloud. "Yes . . . I am. I'm ready . . ."

EIGHT

LITTLE NERD Accountant Girl didn't get the dialogue exactly right, in the movie that she'd play over and over again in her head – it was a little more brusque than that. But she didn't care.

About 5:00 p.m. or so, the company offices starting to close down for the evening – this is maybe a couple of days or so after that last bit, when I'd had to stay so late and cut the check for Cole. I can't remember exactly; that's how excited I got.

Anyway, in this movie – the real one – she looks up and there's Mr. McIntyre standing in her office door again. Be still, my beating heart. Not his big nice-boss smile this time, but just sort of thoughtful and preoccupied.

"Uh, Kim . . ." He gives a little nod. "I've been meaning to talk to you."

"What about, Mr. McIntyre?" She folds her hands on top of the printouts she had been going over, trying not to look any more nervous than she always does.

"We're going to be making some changes around here. I mean, in the Accounting Department. Shift things around a little bit. I just wanted to give you a heads-up, that's all."

"When –" She can barely speak, her heart's wedged up in her throat so tight. "When's this going to happen?"

"Tomorrow, actually. You'll see when you come in. Don't worry about it." Now the big smile. "I'm sure it'll all be something you can get behind. You have a good evening . . ."

An hour later, she's on the bus heading home, and her heart's still pounding away. It's a long ride to get from downtown back over to the crappy neighborhood where I used to live with my little brother Donnie. But this time, she doesn't mind. The bus grinds and crawls along through rush-hour traffic, and all she can see are more of the bright, happy movies playing on the screen inside her head. What a joker her boss is! Something you can get behind – yeah, everything she's ever wanted, that's all. Finally it's happening, after all her hard work, all those late hours. Everything's going to be different now, for both her and Donnie. Real different.

Something outside the bus, in the next lane over, does manage to break through and catch her eye. It's a motorcycle that some guy's riding, zipping through traffic. A little number called a Ninja 250R, made by Kawasaki. Technically a sportbike, though the engine's on the small side: 250 cc displacement, hence the model name. A year ago, she'd had a big adventure – big for her, something that nobody would have figured for the mousy kind of girl that I used to be. She'd actually paid a $100, carefully squeezed out of her bare-bones household budget, and taken the Motorcycle Rider Safety Course over at the community college. For a whole weekend, she'd paddled across a roped-off set of asphalt basketball courts, wearing a borrowed helmet as she and the other students had slowly weaved their way around the orange plastic cones, then eventually getting up to speed – sort of. The bike she'd ridden had been a Ninja 250R, just like the one scooting along outside the bus, only considerably more beat-up. She'd added a couple of scrapes, dropping it just one time. But she'd still managed to pass the course, getting the little piece of paper that she had taken down to the Department of Motor Vehicles office and getting a new driver's license with a little M printed on it. Which she figured meant that she was a motorcyclist, even if she didn't own a motorcycle. She'd made a promise to herself about that, though – When everything changes, when everything's different – justifying it on the basis that not only would it be thrifty urban transportation, it would also show the world that she wasn't just the Little Nerd Accountant Girl everybody thought she was.

I guess the world's pretty much learned that by now, though not exactly the way I had been planning on back then.

Flash-forward in the movie another hour, and now she's sitting on the edge of her brother's bed. The two of them lean their heads together, each stepping on the other's words as they excitedly go over all their plans for the big day tomorrow. The day they always knew was going to come.

"You can't be the new Chief Financial Officer, dressed like that –"

Donnie's only telling her what she already knows. That's why she's carried into the bedroom the special garment bag that she's kept hanging on the wheeled rack out in the living room. The rack's as much of a closet as she has right now. Everything on it is pretty drab, all of her Nerd Accountant Girl stuff, the cheap white blouses, the shapeless skirts – everything, that is, except for the contents of the zippered garment bag. There's just one outfit inside it, that she's carefully collected, bit by bit, as she'd been able to scrape the money together. Then go over to some discount outlet store and try to find something as close as possible to what she and her little brother, leaning over the magazines spread out on his bed, had figured would make her look like a real businesswoman, on her way up the corporate ladder.

Okay, so now the movie isn't some action thing, like it was when Cole was up on the screen, doing his job. Now it's more of a chick flick – working girl transformed to corporate Cinderella – as Donnie and I reinspect the garment bag's contents. There's the tailored pencil skirt that comes up above my knees a carefully calibrated distance more than allowed by those clunky schoolgirl schmattas I had been wearing. The jacket, dark red with three-quarters sleeves, just enough color so it didn't look like a man's. Silk blouse with a lady-lawyer bow at the neck. Nude taupe pantyhose, that a salesgirl had told me would go with an Asian skin tone – those were a completely new thing to me, and kind of scary.

We both sat there on the bed, looking at the clothes. Then I took a deep breath, gathered them all up in my arms, and carried them to the bathroom. Pulling everything on in there was like getting dressed in a phone booth with faucets – I had to sit down on the edge of the tub to put the shoes on. They had two-inch heels, which brought me that much over five feet. Very intimidating. I leaned close to the mirror, working with the nail scissors out of the medicine cabinet, until I had some bangs that I could brush a little to one side, instead of the total skinned-back ponytail look I had been sporting. One of the magazines in our arsenal was a fashion thing for teenagers – younger than me, even – that had an article on how to do that. Which I'd memorized but hadn't pulled the trigger on, until now.

"How's this?"

Donnie studied me critically for a few seconds. His squinting frown made me nervous. This was the first time I'd put every piece on, all at the same time. "Turn around."

I buttoned the jacket and turned my back to him.
"Okay, look at me again."

I turned all the way around, holding my breath.

He regarded me for another couple of seconds, then slowly nodded.

Then smiled.

"Rock 'n' roll," he said, looking me straight in the eye. "Locked and loaded!"

† † †

Of course, one of the problems with giving yourself a complete makeover is that nobody recognizes you when you go to work. I had to dig around in my purse – also a part of the new outfit, instead of the backpack I usually carried – to find my company ID card, to get past the guard in the building lobby.

And then I'm upstairs. Stepping out of the elevator, ready for my new life.

This is a good movie. I'd practiced with the heels back at the apartment, so even those were under control. A couple of moving-type guys carrying cardboard file boxes brushed past me in the hallway. That was a good sign; it meant that things were getting ready for me. I give them a smile; one of them even notices.

I poke my head into my dingy little cubbyhole. Yes! Even more action. Other men in coveralls were packing up all the files, and the computer terminal off the top of my desk. How much more do I need to see?

"Careful with that," I say to the guy lifting the computer. "Lot of important stuff on there."

"Lady –" It's the first time anybody's ever called me that. "My kid's got a better machine than this."

"Your kid doesn't work for Mr. McIntyre," the transformed Nerd Accountant Girl informs him. "We watch our pennies, okay? So just make sure there aren't pieces falling off when it gets over to where it's going."

The movers look at each other and shrug.

Now we do a tracking shot as she heads over to the other side of the building, where McIntyre and the other execs have their offices. It's a lot nicer over there, with potted palms and freshly painted walls, and the kind of framed paintings that you see in expensive hotels rather than Motel 6 lobbies. Even a couple of minor Warhols.

There's a corner office with big tall windows that's been vacant for nearly a year. Because the position had been empty as well. As she comes walking up, she smiles because she sees the workman precisely lettering the position title – CHIEF FINANCIAL OFFICER – on the front of the propped-open door, as the movers carry the file boxes past him. She squeezes by them, careful not to bump the arm of the guy doing the lettering.

Then she halts, right in the middle of the office. There's somebody she's never seen before, sitting behind the desk, his jacket hanging off and hanging on the wooden coat rack by the cabinets. Young guy, with slicked back Gordon Gekko-type hair and an expensive-looking silk necktie. He's sitting there in his shirtsleeves – the shirt looks expensive, too – and he's going over some of the printouts that he's taken from one of the file boxes the movers have stacked up beside the desk.

After a moment, he realizes that there's somebody there, staring at him. He brings his gaze up and looks back at her. "Is there something I can help you with?"

The movie goes into a tight close-up on her. She's not smiling now. "Who are you?"

"Pardon me?"

She feels a little dizzy. Beyond the desk, which is about as big as her old cubbyhole office, the windows look out over a dizzying expanse of the city.

"Okay –" She nods; now she gets it. "Mr. McIntyre didn't tell me that I'd be getting an assistant."

The Brooks Brother guy – that's what she's already calling him, inside her head – frowns in puzzlement. "Assistant? What are you talking about?"

One of McIntyre's officious, snooty secretaries appears in the doorway. "Sorry, Mr. Harris. I didn't see her barge in –"

"Wait a minute." Nerd Accountant Girl turns on the woman. "I didn't 'barge in' anywhere. This is the CFO's office, right? Well, that's me."

The Brooks Brothers guy and the secretary both stare at her. He lowers his head and murmurs softly to the secretary: "Call Security."

"No –" She jabs a finger toward the secretary, who freezes. "Call Mr. McIntyre."

Cut to McIntyre's office. He's sitting behind his even bigger desk, and she's slumped in a chair in front of it. She stares straight ahead of herself, seeing nothing.

"I'm sorry," says McIntyre. "I meant to tell you before."

She doesn't look up. "Tell me what?"

"That I'm not giving you the job. Not the one you apparently thought you were getting, at least."

She stiffens a little bit. "What do you mean?"

McIntyre slowly shakes his head. "Did you really think I was going to make you the company's chief financial officer?"

"Wait a minute." Now she does look up at him. "You told me –"

"Told you what?"

"When I came here. Over a year ago. You told me, that when the company got up and running, that job would be mine."

"Kim –"

"You did. You did tell me that. And now the company is up and running. So who's that in my office?"

McIntyre heaves a sigh. "It's not your office, Kim. It's his. He's my new CFO."

"Are you joking?" Her hands go white-knuckled as she grips the arms of the chair. "He's not any older than me!"

"Well, actually, he is. At least by a couple of years. Plus . . . he's an MBA. Harvard."

"What's that mean? What does he know about running your business?"

He gazes at her sadly for a moment. "He'll learn."

"But I know already!" Her voice rises. This is the most she's ever said in one go, to anybody at the company, let alone the boss. "I know it from the beginning. I know everything. The IRS would've come here, they would've come down on you, if it hadn't –"

"Watch it," growls McIntyre. "Don't even go there."

She doesn't heed the warning. "I did everything for you!" She gets even more emotional. "And you promised me."

"I don't remember saying anything like that." He shrugs. "And if I did – like you said, that was a promise. And this is business. I need that guy."

"Why? Why him and not me?"

"Come on." McIntyre spreads his arms apart. "Be reasonable. It's different now. From what it was even a year ago. Look around you – this isn't some two-bit racket anymore. Some front operation. It's bigger than that now; I've got to have people around me who look right. Who look like him."

She doesn't say anything, but her expression reveals sudden understanding.

"That didn't come out right," says McIntyre. "What I meant was that I need somebody who looks like a Harvard MBA. You can practically smell Harvard on that guy."

"Really?" Her voice is very small and quiet. "And what do I smell like?"

"Look, you're taking this all the wrong way. It's not like I'm firing you; you're just not the CFO. You don't even have to work for the guy; maybe we can send you out to Pomeroy's operation, you can do his accounts –"

"Sure. Or maybe I could park cars down in the garage."

That irritates him. "If you think you could handle it."

And then something happens in that movie I'm telling you, that I'm still amazed about. That I would never have expected from that girl I used to be.

Something snaps in her, and all of a sudden she's up out of that chair, and all 100-whatever pounds of her, in her pathetic little businesswoman getup, are launched across the desk, her hands reaching for McIntyre's throat.

It takes him by surprise as well. He topples backward in his chair, with Little Nerd Accountant Girl on top of him. But it's a pretty uneven fight – soon as he's able to react, all he has to do is backhand her across the face. Then she's down on her knees in front of the desk, sobbing, one hand up to her bloodied mouth. Both of McIntyre's secretaries appear in the doorway and stare wide-eyed at the scene.

He looks over at them. "Get Michael up here."

Michael is the company's head of security. Actually, just a thug who does McIntyre's everyday dirty work, not the hard stuff that Cole takes care of. He's one of those big guys who develop a gut to match their overgrown muscles, and lose their necks in the badly shaved jowls that roll up from their shoulders. He's more than enough to drag Little Nerd Accountant Girl out of the building. Half of him would've been more than enough.

She's still bleeding when Michael tosses her out into the alley behind the building, where the trash dumpsters are lined up.

He squats down on his haunches to look into her bruised face.

"You screwed up big-time, sweetheart." His voice is like tobacco-stained gravel. "And this company doesn't have room for even little screwups. Like you."

He's brought her purse with him. He stands up and tosses it beside her.

"Go home," he tells her.

He turns on his heel and heads back inside the office building, leaving her lying there in the alley . . .

NINE

BIG DEAL, I know. People get fired. I got fired. It happens. Plus – what was I expecting? I was dreaming if I thought that McIntyre was going to make me CFO of his operation. He probably didn't promise it to me; I must've imagined it, dreamed it up in my little schoolgirl head. Even an outfit like that, a total barrel of crooked scams – the only reason he'd had me keeping his books was because he needed some little twit who was so impressed with him that he could push her around, tell her to do things that if I'd been a real accountant, I wouldn't have gone along with in a million years.

I'd known exactly what was going on – I was the one who'd cut the checks to pay his pet hit man. I didn't exactly think Cole was out there selling magazine subscriptions for him. That was why McIntyre had kept me there, crunching his numbers, doing his books. Anybody with any brains – real brains – would've scooted out of there like a shot. But then things changed, and McIntyre had gotten to the point where he could start taking the company legit. That's what smart guys like him do, soon as they get the chance. And then he didn't need somebody like me. He needed a real numbers guy. So he went out and got one. That's all.

Yeah, I had been calling myself an accountant, but I really wasn't one. Not at that age. You have to have qualifications to be one of those – pass tests, get certified and all. I didn't have any of that. I knew how to keep a set of books because a couple of the foster parents that got stuck with me owned a convenience store in Saginaw, Michigan, and the mom showed me how. And I was good at it. Kind of. That's all. Doesn't make me a real accountant. If I was McIntyre, I would've fired my ass, too. Besides . . .

It's not like there weren't other people getting fired.

† † †

Michael, my former boss's chief in-house thug, goes for a drive with Cole, the highly valued freelancer who takes care of the tough jobs that a bullethead like Michael can't be trusted doing. Not in the blazing yellow '57 Bel Air, but one of the company cars. There's a little errand that McIntyre has asked Cole to help Michael out with.

Of course, Cole's happy to oblige. He liked getting under Michael's skin. He told me as much, later on.

Michael's driving, obviously stewing about life in general and how unfair it is for even a bruised-knuckles side-of-beef like himself. His eyes are just two little slits in his scowling face. The relationship between him and Cole is a constant irritation, not the least because he knows that Cole could kill him in about a minute, if he wanted to. So the only thing keeping him alive, Michael knows, is that his boss McIntyre finds him useful around the company building.

Which they're heading away from at the moment. This would probably be a couple of hours after Michael, big strong man that he is, tossed out into the alley the Little Nerd Accountant Girl who had thought she was going to be the new CFO. Real tough guy, all right; give him a 100-pound girl to bring the hammer down on, and he's in his element.

"Heard you had some excitement today." Cole needles him about exactly that. "With our little number-cruncher."

Michael shrugs his beefy shoulders as he drives. "No big deal." Yeah, for him.

"Kind of a shame." Cole leans his elbow on the passenger's side window sill and watches the office buildings slide by. "She wasn't a bad kid. I kinda liked her."

That was something else he told me later. I'd had no idea. I was so terrified and repulsed by him back then.

Michael keeps driving, doesn't say anything except one of his trademark monosyllabic grunts.

"So now who do we get paid by?"

"New system," says Michael. "Because of the company getting all reorganized."

"Yeah?" Cole glances over at him. "What new system?"

"Direct deposit into your bank account. The money just shows up. You'll love it."

"Yeah, right." Cole is unimpressed. "Next you'll tell me we've got dental and a 401(k) now."

"Not for you," says Michael. "You're an independent contractor, remember?"

Cole just shakes his head in disgust and looks away again.

Michael finally pulls the company car up outside a liquor store in one of the city's shabbier neighborhoods. The kind of neighborhood where all the businesses, what few there are, have security ironwork over the windows, including this one. Behind the wheel, Michael nods toward the building. The car stops outside the store.

"No biggie," says Michael. "Just put a scare in him. So he'll know it's not a good idea to be late making his payments."

"Are you kidding?" Cole looks even more disgusted. "This is a waste of my time. Even you could scare this guy."

"McIntyre wanted you to do it." The flame under Michael's simmering scowl gets turned up a notch. "So just take care of it, all right?"

Cole shrugs. "You're the boss." He pushes open the car door.

Michael stays in the company car and watches, leaning his head down, as Cole goes inside the store. Cole starts out easy with the elderly store-owner behind the counter, but the old guy knows what he's there for. The store-owner starts to wave his hands around, all agitated. Cole just shakes his head, then reaches inside his jacket and pulls out the big ugly .357, which he points at the guy.

Out in the car, Michael sees what Cole doesn't. There's a teenage kid, wearing an apron, who's come out of the back of the store, carrying a shotgun. He sneaks down an aisle toward the cash register counter.

Instinctively, Michael's hand moves toward the steering wheel, to honk the horn and warn Cole. But his hand stops an inch short; then he slowly pulls it back.

Inside the liquor store, Cole suddenly glances over his shoulder, but too late. The teenager blasts away, hitting Cole in the small of the back. He collapses right there on the floor.

Everything goes all distorted and weird-angled, the way movies do when somebody's been badly hurt, but somehow they're still conscious. Or at least a little bit.

Through a blurring haze, Cole looks up at the store-owner and the teenager. The echo of the shotgun blast seems to roll on and on. He rolls over on his chest and starts crawling toward the door, his legs dragging behind him.

He gets as far as the sidewalk. Lying in a widening pool of blood, Cole rolls over on his back and sees Michael standing above him. Michael sadly shakes his head.

"You screwed up, man." Michael's voice is all echoey and faint, coming from a million miles away. "Big time."

The movie fades to black as Cole loses it, letting go of everything . . .

TEN

I WASN'T thinking about Cole – at least not back then. I had my own problems to take care of. Of course, some of them were problems I was making for myself.

That's what sucks about having your head in a bad place – which is what happens when something really crappy happens to you, out of the blue. You got a long way to go before you're out of that bad zone. And you might not make it out; some people don't. They just die there. That's something you want to try and avoid.

I wasn't doing a good job of that, after McIntyre fired me, and his pet thug Michael threw me out in the alley behind the office building like I was a sack of garbage. Sure, maybe I hadn't gotten set up to get blown away with a shotgun, the way Michael was going to do to Cole, but I was still seriously screwed up. I didn't know exactly who I was more pissed at – McIntyre for not giving me the CFO job, or myself for having ever imagined that he would. In my wordless, seething rage, with the whole world spinning around me as I picked myself up and walked away from the office building, it finally came down to me. That's who I was furious at. You can hate somebody who screws you over, but there's nobody you want to rip the head off like that fool wearing your face, who answers to your name.

That's probably why I did what I did next. Because I just didn't care what happened to me after that. That's the really bad place you don't want to be in. Because if you want the world to punish you for your sins – believe me, the world will oblige. Happily.

You don't have to take those kinds of sleeping pills – the ones with the TV commercials where they warn you that you might wind up naked, peeing on yourself at the side of the interstate, and getting into a fight with a couple of Highway Patrol officers – to have a blackout and find yourself doing something you wouldn't ordinarily do. Just get your head in that spot and, boom, it happens. Or at least it did for me.

Somehow, after I got tossed out in the alley, I started walking, just walking, not even looking where I was going, bumping into people in a daze – or maybe I got on the bus, any bus; I don't remember. But I wound up someplace I'd been to only one time before, right after I passed the motorcycle course. There's a Kawasaki dealership out on the side of the city, right where the interstate veers off. I'd gone out there and sat on the motorcycle I wanted, a Ninja 250R just like the one I'd learned to ride on, except for it being all new and shiny instead of scuffed up from klutzes like me dropping it on its side. The sales guys probably thought I looked cute – well maybe a little, at least – sitting on top of a zippy little sportbike like that. And they all had agreed that yeah, a half-pint like me was better off with something light and maneuverable, rather than some monster Harley or Goldwing. I'd come home with every color brochure they had, and Donnie and I had spent a happy evening looking at them spread out on top of his bed.

That's where I wound up, in my post-firing fugue state. At the motorcycle dealership. My head was still in that bad space, where I just didn't care. I must've been walking and talking like a normal human being, or close to, but really – I was just along for the ride at that point. Worse luck for me, they had a used 250R that had just shown up as a trade-in. Less than a year old, low miles, perfect condition. And priced right at two-and-a-half grand, which was just about what I had in the money market account that was all the savings Donnie and I had in the world.

As a general rule, you'll find the sales guys at motorcycle stores to be very helpful about impulse purchases. It's their job.

A call to my bank to verify the check I wrote, and I was the new owner of the 250R plus a plain white, full-face HJC helmet, the cheapest one they had in the shop that fit me. Good guys – they wouldn't let me ride the bike off the lot without the helmet.

Which was the only piece of luck I had that day. Because I went down. Hard.

Not actually my fault, but that doesn't matter. I got off to a wobbling start, heading away from the dealership. Missed the first couple of upshifts, almost killed the engine, then whatever muscle memory remained in my body from the rider course kicked in, and I was able to keep rolling. Keeping up with traffic, the skirt of what was supposed to have been my climbing-the-corporate-ladder CFO outfit climbing up my thighs, the two-inch heels hooked over the bike's pegs, my right hand rolling on the throttle. Nobody can see me crying behind the helmet's silvery visor . . .

Here's my advice. If you take nothing else away from this movie, take this much. Don't ride emotional. Don't ride happy, don't ride sad, don't ride with anything else going on inside your head. Don't even think. Just ride. Then you have at least a fighting chance against all those morons on the road.

Things aren't going bad enough for me already, some idiot in a Celica decides to change two lanes in one swoop – not right in front of me, but in front of the panel truck ahead. The driver of which has no choice but to slam on his brakes to avoid hitting the schmuck. All of a sudden, I'm seeing a pair of double doors heading straight into the Ninja's abbreviated windshield. My reflexes kick in without thinking, I'm piling on both the front and rear brakes, I'm good, I'm going to pull it out with maybe a foot to spare between me and the panel truck's rear bumper –

Then my rear wheel hits an oil patch on the asphalt, and I'm not so good.

I can feel a little shudder coming up through the bike seat and into the base of my spine. Somehow, without this ever having happened to me before, I know what this means. My fists tighten on the handlebar grips. A second later, and the rear wheel loses it and comes slewing around toward the front. The only lucky break I get is that instcad of taking a high-sider over the bars, I get whipped around low, the bike going in one direction and me going in another.

Let me tell you what happens when you hit the road at about forty miles per hour –

You bounce.

This might not count as one of the action parts of the movie playing on the screen inside your head. I mean yeah, a motorcycle accident and a body flying through the air – that would be me – and slamming into the asphalt. Because it all seemed strangely . . . tranquil . . . when it happened. Like it really was just happening in a movie, one that I was watching rather than living. One moment I'm on the bike, grabbing a handful of brakes, then I'm flying, and then I'm piling into the ground shoulder-first. I don't even feel anything; it's all strangely painless. Then I'm up in the air again. I'm looking at the sky, and it's so intensely blue, even through the helmet's tinted visor, that it's a revelation.

I'm glad I got to see that. Though I still don't know exactly what it means.

Then I'm on my back, and I'm aware of cars stopped around me and my motorcycle lying on its side a couple of yards away. The driver of the car that had been behind me, who was gracious enough not to run over me when I went down, is bending over me and asking if I'm all right.

If they weren't before, by this time the pantyhose are definitely goners. I've got a scraped knee oozing blood, but I'm able to sit up and pull off my helmet.

"I'm fine –" A strange exhilaration fills me, maybe just because I'm still alive. "It's okay."

"You sure?"

"Yes." I nod. I've managed to get to my feet. Everything seems to be working, and the world tilts back to level. "My Ninja –"

The car driver peers at me. "Your what?" The other driver, the moron who caused the accident, is long gone by now.

"My motorcycle –" I'm more concerned about it than myself. "Over there –"

He helps me pick it up and roll it over to the side of the road. Now that I'm out of the way instead of lying in the middle of the lane like a doormat, traffic resumes rolling by.

He watches me try to brush myself off. "You need to go to the hospital."

Yeah, right. Like I've got insurance. That's just one more thing I was hoping to get with my promotion to CFO.

"I'm fine." There's blood on one of my palms as well, where I had scraped my hand on the asphalt. "Seriously."

"Seriously, my butt." He's really concerned. He picks up my helmet from where I had set it down on the curb. "Look at this." He shows me the side of the helmet, where it's all crumpled and dented, like a hard-boiled egg that's been dropped on the kitchen floor. "You need to go in and have X-rays done."

I reach up and touch my head, right above one ear. My fingertips come away wet and red. I wipe them on my dirty, scuffed-up skirt. "It's nothing."

The car driver takes a cell phone from his pocket. "I'm calling nine-one-one."

"No –" I grab his hand before he can punch in the numbers. "Don't. I'll be all right –"

He studies me for a few seconds, then shrugs and puts the phone away. "Your funeral, lady." He gets back into his car and drives away. That's the last I see of him.

So that leaves me on the side of the road. I'm a sight, my business-lady outfit looking like it had been used to mop up a garage floor, my face streaked with dust and tears, blood caking and drying at the side of my head. The motorcycle looks better than I do. The right-side fairing is scraped down to the fiberglass, or plastic or whatever it's made out of, and there's a crack in the upper corner of the windshield, but basically it's all holding together pretty well. Tough little machine – no wonder they're popular.

Of course, after a fall like that, I'm not going to climb back on top of the Ninja and ride away. I'm too spooked, hands shaking so badly that I wouldn't be able to keep a grip on the handlebars. I'm not going to leave it there, though. Good thing it's so lightweight, as the upshot of my decision is that I'm going to have to wheel it home. Which is where I must've been heading in my whacked-out fugue state. I look around and recognize the local landmarks, the store on the corner, that sort of thing, and realize I'm maybe ten, twelve blocks away from the shabby apartment building where Donnie and I live. That's another break, at least.

And talking about spooked – something weird happens as I'm getting ready to make the trek. I'm still rattled by what happened – maybe bonking my head on the asphalt did knock something loose inside my skull. Maybe a slight concussion? You know you're screwed when you're hoping for it, when something like that would be the good news compared to what else might be wrong. If I woke up dead tomorrow morning, I wouldn't be surprised. Right now, I wasn't even all that upset at the prospect, except for worrying about who would take care of Donnie if I were vanished from the scene.

The weird thing – I take a deep breath, trying to pull myself together as much as I can. Standing at the side of the motorcycle, I pull it up straight with its handlebars and lift the kickstand out of the way with the toe of one badly scuffed shoe. As I'm doing all that, a strange perception washes over me, as though all the surrounding buildings, and the cars zooming by on the road a few feet away from me, were all just painted on overlapping transparent sheets. As though none of them were real, with no actual substance to them, just their flat two-dimensional appearances being all that they possessed. That made me feel even more disconnected. For a moment, I was actually afraid that a wind would pick up and scatter the transparencies with the buildings and the cars and everything else on them – leaving behind what? I didn't know. Didn't want to find out, either.

I took another deep breath and the disoriented perception faded a bit, as though reality was seeping back into the two-dimensional things around me, filling them out, making them real again. But not before I had one other freaky perception, that scared me even more. For just a second, I had the strangest feeling of being watched, and from every direction – as though those transparent sheets with the buildings and cars on them suddenly raised a little bit from their lower corners. And there were things peering out from behind them, their blank eyes narrowing first with curiosity, then darkening with some unfathomable intent directed toward me.

By that point, I was thinking maybe I should get over to an emergency room and have my head x-rayed.

The weird perception passed and the world became normal around me again, all solid the way it had been before. It still sucked, but at least it sucked in the way that I had become used to.

It must've taken me an hour, but I got myself and the motorcycle home at last. Now I was even more sore and weary, from the effort of keeping the machine upright and pushing it along, from one long block to the next. But the fatigue helped numb the other pain, at least.

I left the motorcycle parked at the curb in front of the building. I'd have to make other arrangements for it, and soon. In this crappy neighborhood, you couldn't leave anything like that hanging around in the open, without one of our lovely neighbors making off with it. I'd have to go back to the dealership and get one of those heavy-duty chains they sell just for locking up motorcycles, with the big heavy links that can't be cut with anything short of military ordnance. I figured the bike could make it through one night before it was in real danger of disappearing. And if it did vanish, at this point I didn't know whether I even cared. About it or anything else.

Of course, that was the bad place talking, inside my head. But that's where I was.

I climbed up the four flights of stairs to our tiny apartment. Donnie heard me letting myself in and called out from the bedroom at the back. "Kimmie? That you?"

I dropped the business-lady purse on the kitchenette table – the purse didn't look brand-new and professional anymore, either. It had also taken a hard shot in the fall, out on the street. I morosely ran a fingertip across the raw scrape in what had been nice shiny leather, while wondering just what I was going to tell my younger brother.

This took even more gathering up what little strength I had left. All the way home, pushing the motorcycle along, this was what I hadn't allowed myself to think about.

"Kimmie?"

I took one last deep breath, drawing my hand away from the scuffed-up purse on the little table. There was a hard knot of something in my gut, that I could use to walk back to the bedroom where Donnie was waiting for me. It wasn't courage or resolve or anything good like that. Maybe it was just resignation, the notion that at least I'd gotten to a point where things couldn't get any worse.

Of course, I was wrong about that. But finding it out came later.

I walked down the little hallway to the bedroom, pushed open the door, and stood there. I didn't say anything, but just let him look at me. And the condition I was in.

"Kimmie –" His eyes widened. "What happened to you?"

This was supposed to have been the moment when I came home and told him about all the wonderful things that were happening out there in the world, and all the wonderful things that were going to happen. For both of us.

Instead, I sat down on the edge of the mattress and reached over and wrapped my arms around him. Then I was rocking both of us back and forth, holding onto him as tight as I could. As though I was afraid that this was going to be taken away from me, too. The way I knew in my heart that it would be, some time that I didn't let myself think about.

"I had a bad day." I couldn't stop myself from pressing my face to his skinny little shoulder and sobbing. "I had a real bad day."

ELEVEN

LET ME tell you some more stuff you probably already know. I mean, this is stuff that everybody in the world seemed to already know, and I was just late coming to the party.

When it takes a motorcycle accident to knock some sense into your head, you're right in thinking that you've been kind of an idiot most of your life.

That wasn't what I wanted to tell you. This is it, actually: the real problem with getting your head into the bad place, whatever it happens to be for you – your stupid boyfriend, your crappy marriage, your job (none of which were things that I was worrying about at the moment), whatever – is that one bad decision just leads to another.

You have to work to break that cycle. And some people never do.

You should try not to be one of those people.

That's what I was finally trying, sitting out in the front room of the tiny apartment the next morning, after a long, sleepless, and crying night. My face was still all reddened and puffy, way after the tears had finally stopped. If you haven't already noticed, that's what kind of a wuss I was.

"Maybe I could sell it."

"Sell what?" Donnie was in his wheelchair, across from me, so close that our knees were touching underneath the table we ate at.

"The motorcycle." I pointed to the window. "Maybe I could go back to the dealership and return it. Get my money back."

"I don't know . . ." He pushed himself up, so he could look out the window again. That was why he'd gotten into the wheelchair – it took a little doing, on both our parts – so he could come out and see it, parked down at the curb in front of the apartment building. "It looks kinda banged-up."

"It runs." The scraped fairing was even more evident in the morning light. "At least I think it does."

He knew better than to ask about insurance. That would've been a joke.

"No." Donnie shook his head. "You should keep it."

"Why?"

"Simple." He looked into my face and shrugged. "It's what you always wanted."

"That's not good enough. We still have to pay the rent." Which, even on a dump like this, was a scary amount. "And eat." I didn't say anything about his medications. "What're we going to do for money?"

That was the real problem with the bad space that I'd let both of us get dragged into. It's always money, when you come right down to it.

What I'd spent buying the Ninja had drained our savings right down to the low two-digit marker. The shallower that particular pool got, the easier it was to drown in it. That was all we had in this world. Which was okay, while I was still working and covering our monthly nut with what McIntyre paid me. And now that was done.

"I don't have a job now, Donnie. That was where the paychecks came from. Remember?"

"You can get another one. Another job."

The kid had confidence, all right. That was a good attitude for him to have, when it hooked up with his getting better someday. But right now, being confident in his older sister didn't seem like the smartest bet to make.

"Sure," I said. "And I will. But that might take a while. They don't exactly grow on trees nowadays."

"So . . ." He nodded, looking all sage and wise. "We just need something to tide us over. Get us by for a while. Right?"

"You got it, pal."

"Okay, then." He smiled. "There's something you're forgetting. You always forget it."

"What, the plasma donor center?" That was a running joke with us, especially around Christmas time. "There's not enough blood in both of us put together to buy a ham sandwich with."

At least I had gotten back to the point where I could kid around with my brother. I still felt like crap, but that much of me was functioning. I even managed a weak little smile.

"No, stupid." He gave a shake of his head. "The envelope. You always forget the envelope."

That much, smart as he was, he was wrong about. I didn't forget about it. I just didn't want to remember it. There's a difference.

"Donnie." I wasn't smiling now. "We made a pact. We weren't going to touch that. We weren't even going to talk about it."

"Yeah, but that was before. Now is different."

He had a point. More than he probably realized.

It wasn't just the money thing – not having it, that is – that made now different. It was what had happened inside my head.

I was still getting that weird feeling, that crazy perception, that everything I saw outside was painted on transparent sheets, laid one on top of another. All two-dimensional and phony. Something that could be blown away by a good strong wind. I looked out the apartment's smudged, dust-covered window. In some ways, everything looked like it had before; in some essential way it was all different, like bad special effects that you see in a cheap action movie.

And I wasn't even sure what was going on inside my head that would cause that feeling. I was pretty sure I was recovered from the fall on the motorcycle, other than some impressively picturesque bruises running down along my ribs and onto my hip on the side I had landed on. I had taken a shower that morning, mainly to wash the dried blood out of my hair. When I was done, I had managed to inspect my skinny naked body in the mirror over the sink and discovered that a big stretch of me didn't look Asian anymore – it looked like some bad modern-art painting.

It'd be a while before that faded. Felt tender, also. Which, thankfully, at least my head no longer did. Wrapped up in a towel, I had leaned close to the mirror and taken a few tentative fingertip pokes at the side of my head. Nothing seemed broken, at least not that I could tell. That was as much diagnostic work as I could afford at the moment, other than holding my head up to a real bright light and asking Donnie if he could see anything suspicious.

The spooky two-dimensional thing came and went, though, so I tried just not to think about it. A little more difficult with the bit about things looking at me from underneath the edges of the clear plastic sheets on which the world seemed to be painted. That creeped me out a lot more.

As to the cause of those weird feelings, that was just one more thing not to think about. If it wasn't an after-effect of the motorcycle accident – like I said, I felt like I had pretty much recovered from it – then the only other thing was all the other crap that had happened yesterday. Not just getting fired, but finding out that everything I had been dreaming about had been a joke on me. That and getting tossed out into the alley like a bag of trash. If that was what had screwed my head up, made the whole world seem two-dimensional and fake, and not just getting my head slammed onto the road . . .

Then that wasn't good. Even less good than everything else that wasn't good in my life right now. If that was the cause, then I was pretty sure it was going to take a lot longer to get over than the whack to the skull.

Meanwhile, there were more bad things – bad ideas – happening in that bad space where my head was at.

Like the envelope.

Even if Donnie had brought it up – I was still the older one. I was the big sister. As close to an adult as our little family unit had – or had had for a long time. I could've put the kibosh on that whole notion, if I'd wanted to . . .

But I didn't.

I just sat there on my side of the table for a couple of minutes, not saying anything, just staring in front of myself. Trying to keep the world inside my head from falling part.

"All right," I said at last. "What do you think we should do?"

"Kimmie –" My younger brother regarded me with great sad seriousness. "We don't even know what's in it."

I nodded slowly. He was right about that.

So the first step, the first thing we had to do right now, was find out what we were actually talking about. Maybe there wasn't even anything to be scared about at all.

I pushed the wobbly wooden chair back and stood up from the table. I went to Donnie's bedroom and to the closet at the far end of it. Up on the top shelf was where I stored the big heavy sweaters we wore around the apartment at night, even sleeping in them when the winter weather got really cold, because the landlord shut off the heat at 9:00 p.m. Underneath the sweaters was the envelope, right where I had hidden it. I stood on my tiptoes and pulled it out, then stood there looking at it in my hand. A plain white envelope, the kind you'd stick a stamp on and mail a letter to your grandmother with, if you had one. Only this envelope was fat and heavy with whatever it was stuffed with.

Twisted around in the wheelchair, Donnie watched me as I carried the envelope out of the bedroom and set it down in the center of the table. Carefully, as if it were a bomb.

I sat down again. We both looked at the envelope there between us. Then Donnie looked up at me.

"Kimmie," he said. "You have to open it."

I nodded, took a deep breath, then picked up the envelope. I slid my fingertip under the corner of the sealed flap, then tore it open.

"Wow," said Donnie after a moment. "That's a lot."

He was right. I sat there looking at all the money filling the envelope. Without even taking it out and counting it, I had to agree.

It was a lot.

† † †

Now you're really thinking about what kind of idiot I must be.

First, I convince myself that some heavyweight guy like McIntyre is going to make some little nothing like me into the Chief Financial Officer for all his businesses, both the legal and illegal ones. So it winds up taking me completely by surprise when he has me tossed out into the alley behind the office building, when he no longer has any use for me. Anybody with a brain – which seems to leave me out – could've seen that coming.

And then after that, I'm sitting in our crappy little apartment that I don't even know how I'm going to pay next month's rent on, and I've got an envelope stuffed with money in my hands – big money; I can see $100 bills in there – and I'm about ready to pass out from fear.

Yeah, what does it take to make a girl happy these days?

So here's the story about the envelope. And why I'm not a complete idiot to have butterflies zooming through my stomach like a bomber squadron.

A month before, and of course I'm still working for Mr. McIntyre. Droning away, Little Nerd Accountant Girl, dreaming of my big break that I was just sure was going to come any day now. A bright future, yadda yadda. And I'm there in my little windowless cubbyhole late at night, grinding over the books, like so many times before. I really am the only one left there, except for the janitors polishing the building's lobby floor –

A guy that everybody calls Badooch shows up in my office doorway. He actually has some Italian last name, but nobody calls him by that; they call him Badooch instead. He doesn't seem to mind. Young, twitchy guy, always fidgeting and looking over his shoulder at something or someone who isn't there. He scares me – but that's no big deal, since little Nerd Accountant Girl is scared of everything, including her own shadow. But there is an atmosphere of random violence that seems to sweat out of his pores, like the chemical residue of whatever it is he's always so cranked up on.

"Take care of this for me, will ya?" He stays in the doorway rather than stepping into my tiny office, as though it's some kind of trap. From there, he tosses a plain white letter-sized envelope onto my desk. Yes, it's that envelope. "Just route it over to McIntyre when you get a chance."

Then he's gone, slipping out of the building without even saying thanks to me. Nobody ever did.

I'm not so scared of the guy that as soon as he's gone, I don't get sulky and resentful about being asked to do something right when I'm packing up and getting ready to go home. So instead of dialing up the combination on my desk's bottom drawer, which I've already closed and locked, I just stuff the fat envelope into my backpack, turn off the lights, and head for the elevator.

Stupid as I am back then, I'm not even thinking about what might possibly be in the envelope. I know that Badooch is actually a courier for the branch operation that his immediate boss Pomeroy runs for Mr. McIntyre. And Pomeroy is in the habit of folding up all sorts of multipage reports and bundles of receipts, then sending them over like that. I figure this one is also something of the sort. No big deal.

Matter of fact, it's such a non-deal to me that I completely forget about the envelope in my backpack. I don't remember it at all until I hear that thug Michael talking to one of the other security guards, in the hallway outside my cubbyhole. They would never keep their voices down, since for them I didn't really exist at all.

"Find him yet?" That was Michael buttonholing the other security guy.

"Nope." The other one shook his head. "I've got all sorts of people out on the street, asking if anybody's seen Badooch – so far, nothing. Complete nada."

"Damn." Michael was all kinds of irritated.

"You know what I think?" The other security guy sounded hyped-up. "Badooch had a lot of enemies. He really had a knack for getting people mad. I think somebody iced him."

"Wouldn't be surprised." I could see Michael's big ugly face go all brooding. "Little bastard could've swung by here and made his delivery before getting himself killed. That would've been nice."

The two men had walked away, still talking about unpleasant things. And my mind had started racing.

In my backpack was the delivery that they were talking about. The envelope that Badooch had tossed onto my desk – that must be it. Michael and everybody else – they didn't know that Badooch had come by after hours and given the envelope to me, before he got himself erased off the face of the earth. For all they knew, whoever had iced him – to use their charming phrase – had thrown him and the envelope he had been carrying in his jacket into the same hole they'd dug for him, or under the same bridge on the river. They didn't know I had it.

Which made a problem for me. I had been holding on to the envelope for two days now, while everybody had been searching for the vanished courier. I was still thinking I had a shot at going from grunt accountant to the company's Chief Financial Officer – more than a shot; I thought it was a sure thing. That was mainly what I didn't want to screw up. I didn't care what was in the envelope sitting at the bottom of my backpack –

though I was already starting to think it might not be just paperwork. And here I had been waltzing in and out of the building with it, for two days now. That looked bad – real bad. I was supposed to be detail-oriented, executive material, and here I was schlepping around with something that I shouldn't even have taken with me in the first place. I should've locked it up in my desk, then gotten it to McIntyre first thing the next morning. And I had screwed that up, without even intending to. Not good.

I didn't know what to do. And neither did my younger brother – I always talked over things like this with him, when I got home. But he didn't have a clue as to a course of action, either.

Naturally, what I should've done is go right on in to McIntyre's office and 'fess up, tell him what happened, herc's the envelope – he and I would've had a good laugh about it all. In fact, he would've been so impressed with my honesty and what a loyal, hardworking employee I was, he would've made me CFO right there on the spot, instead of waiting for the big corporate reorganization he was planning. That's exactly what would've happened – right after every flying pig in the universe came in for a landing on the aircraft carrier deck of my overheated schoolgirl imagination.

But I didn't do that. That didn't happen.

Instead, I spent the next day and the day after that, even more scared and mousy at work. The plain white envelope was still there in my backpack – I didn't even dare touch it. And then a week had gone by, and nobody had said anything to me about Badooch having given me the envelope before he disappeared, and then another week went by.

I hadn't been able to stand it any more. The tension had my gut in a knot even tighter than it usually was. I finally sat down at the kitchenette table and pulled the envelope out of my backpack. Donnie had been sitting there in his wheelchair, and he had watched me do it. He had looked at the sealed envelope, how thick and fat and heavy it was, then he had looked up at me. Our eyes had met, with the envelope trembling in my hands, and a little message had silently passed between us. We both had known what was in it.

And what would happen now, if anybody found out I had it . . .

† † †

That was the envelope I had just dug out from underneath the sweaters in the bedroom closet. That I had just torn open, so that Donnie and I could see all the money inside it.

I turned the envelope upside down and dumped out its contents, a green haystack in the center of the table.

It took us a while to count it all. Then recount it.

I sat back in my chair, stunned. I looked up and saw Donnie smiling at me.

"Well," he said. "I guess we don't have to worry about paying the rent for a while."

TWELVE

"OKAY," I TOLD Donnie. "We have to be careful about this. We have to be smart."

We sat there with the lights switched off, the curtains already drawn before I had torn open the envelope. Two conspirators without a plan, their minds racing. Mine felt like a white rat sprinting inside of those wheels that go round and round without ever arriving anywhere, but unable to stop or even slow down.

"I know," said Donnie. His smile was gone now. I could tell that he had been thinking. And hard. "If we're not smart, we'll be dead."

That was one way of putting it.

"Here's what we should do." Little Nerd Accountant Girl had also been thinking. "We can't just spend it. I mean, spend a lot of it. Just as little of it as we can, just to get by. Right?"

In deep serious mode, my younger brother nodded.

"The less of it we spend, the less likely anybody will know we have it." I leaned over the stacks of bills. "That's the main thing."

"Do you think they're watching you?"

"I don't know," I said. "I don't think so. When Mr. McIntyre had me tossed out – that was probably the end of it as far as he was concerned." I could still remember the disgusted look on my former boss's face, as if I had been literally transformed into a sack of overripe trash. Fit for nothing now, except being taken to the dumpsters out in the alley. "He probably doesn't even know I exist anymore."

"Are you sure?"

"I told you – I don't know." The rat was running even faster inside his little wheel. And still not getting anywhere. "That's why we have to be careful. He doesn't care enough to have me watched – but there might be somebody around here who works for him, or who knows somebody who does." In this neighborhood, that was highly likely. "Somebody like that sees us acting like we have a lot of money, they know I used to work for Mr. McIntyre, they know I got fired, they think about it –" The rat was going so fast, I was practically hysterical. I gripped the edge of the table with both hands and took a deep breath, trying to calm myself. "They'd go and tell him, wouldn't they? And he might figure it out, where that money had come from. This money. And then we'd be in trouble. Big trouble."

"Okay." Donnie nodded. "I understand."

Little Nerd Account Girl – or that person who used to be her and was now already in the process of becoming me – sat there staring at the money for a couple minutes longer, before she spoke again.

"We can't just pick up and leave," I said. "That wouldn't do us any good. If Mr. McIntyre decides he wants to find us, then he can find us. Wherever we go."

"Sure –" Donnie was tuning into the wavelength of this new world in which we had found ourselves. "We're safer right here where we are. 'Cause they wouldn't expect us to do that, if they thought we had their money. Stay right here, I mean. They'd expect us to run away. So that's exactly what we can't do."

"Right." The rat was now approaching Mach speed inside its little wheel. "So we have to stay right here. And not spend any of the money, except what we absolutely have to. Okay?"

He nodded. "Okay." There was a wheel spinning inside his head, too. I could see it behind his eyes. "So you gotta be doing whatever you'd be doing if you didn't have this money. Right?"

"What . . ." My turn for a slow nod. "What would that be?"

"A job," said Donnie. "That's what you were already thinking you had to do. Go out looking for another job."

This is an indication of what a crummy world we live in. Here I get thrown out on my ear like a sack of trash, I get my head whanged in a motorcycle accident, there's a pile of money on the table in front of me, that I'll get killed over if anybody finds out it's here – and I still don't get to take any time off. What do you have to do to get a vacation these days?

"All right." My nod became even slower and more deliberate. "I'll start tomorrow. I mean – that's what I would've been doing, anyway."

I piled up the money and slid it all back into the envelope. At least we had a plan now.

The only problem – it just wasn't a very good one.

As I found out . . .

† † †

"Do us both a favor, sweetheart." The bartender looked up at me, as he was polishing a glass with a towel. "Just turn around and leave."

I stood right there in front of him. "Why?"

"Are you kidding?" He inspected the glass, holding it up and turning it in the light, then picked up another one. "Look at you. You're so far under-age, it's illegal for you to even be thinking about coming into a place like this. And spare me whatever phony ID you've got in your purse. I don't want to see it."

With some black shoe polish, I had managed to get the purse part of my business-lady getup into presentable condition again. As long as nobody looked too hard at me. The jacket and the skirt took some more doing, but at least I could go out in public with them. I'd picked up another pair of panty hose at the drugstore on the corner, then slipped into a gas station ladies' room to pull them on before heading to the first stop on my list.

"What's the big deal?" I never used to talk like that, when I had still been Little Nerd Accountant Girl. Maybe it was the whack on the head. "You're not even open." The chairs were stacked upside-down on the bar's tables. "And I don't want a drink."

"So what do you want?"

"I want to talk to the manager."

He eyed me with suspicion. "What about?"

"A job."

"You gotta be kidding." He pointed to the stage at the side of the bar, with the brass stripper pole bolted to the floorboards and the ceiling, up by the switched-off lights. "I don't know what you've heard at whatever high school you should be in right now, but you gotta be of age to do that, too. Come back in a few years. Or better yet, don't bother." He smiled as he looked me over. "You're not exactly cut out for the gig, if you get what I mean. Don't take it personal – it's just reality."

That reality was something I was already familiar with. What he meant was that I didn't have the natural talents – or implants; same thing – and general air of predatory sexuality possessed by the woman with long red hair down her back, sitting over by the stage, moodily reading a newspaper with her arms over the back of the chair. She looked like a hard number, but I could imagine that she did pretty well from the tips that would get stuffed into her garter belt whenever she was performing.

"That's not the job I want." Did I really have to tell this guy that? "Look, is the manager in or not? I just want to talk to him. And then I'll get out of your hair."

"Okay, okay. If it's that important —"

He came out from behind the bar and led me over to a door at the side, way past the restrooms.

"Mr. Stavros?"

"Do I know you?" The balding guy behind the desk, with the papers spread out all over it, along with a copy of The Daily Racing Form, looked up at me. "If you're selling Girl Scout cookies, I'm only interested in the Thin Mints. Those, I like."

"Maybe you remember me," I said. "We met when you came over to McIntyre's offices. A couple of months ago. There was some mix-up with the rental agreement for this place, and I went over the payments ledger with you —"

"Oh, yeah." He nodded. "Now I recall it. Kathy, right?"

"Kim, actually."

"Sorry. I meet a lot of young women in this business. Hard to remember all their names. But I remember you. You were a lot of help. My butt was in a jam."

"Kind of." I gave him a smile. "Took some doing, but we got it all straightened out."

The man had reason for remembering me with some degree of gratitude. I really had bailed him out back then. There had been some confusion about a missed lease payment, and for some reason Mr. McIntyre had gotten all pissed off about it, to the point of having Michael hanging outside my cubbyhole while I had gone over the books with the sweating bar manager sitting in front of me. Just as if Michael was going to rip the guy's head off if every nickel wasn't accounted for. I'd finally found the missing money – the guy who'd been taking care of the bar and nightclub accounts before I took over had misfiled a couple of checks – and I had phoned up to McIntyre's office and explained everything. Michael had slunk off down the hallway like a Rottweiler who'd been deprived of an anticipated bone. The bar manager had smoothed his unraveling comb-over back across his brown-spotted scalp and told me that if I ever needed a favor, to look him up.

That's what I was doing now.

"So what can I do for you?" He pointed to the chair at the side of his desk. "Have a seat." A flicker of concern shaded his eyes for a moment. "Nothing wrong back at the office, is there?"

"I wouldn't know." I set my purse on my lap. "I don't work there anymore."

"Oh." With obvious discomfort, he fiddled with a pen on top of the papers. "Guess it's true then, huh?"

"What is?"

"Well . . ." His rounded shoulders lifted in a shrug. "I'd heard there'd been a big shake-up over there. Guess they call that sort of thing a reorganization now, huh? We used to just call it giving people the boot. I think that was better, instead of being all pussyfoot about stuff like that. Anyway, the word's out that McIntyre's going all corporate and stuff. That's his business, I suppose."

I didn't like the sound of what I was hearing. The word being out and all that. "Could I ask what else you heard?" I was still being all polite and Nerd Accountant Girl-ish. "I mean . . . if it's something you feel you can tell me . . ."

"Yeah, well . . . it's not exactly good, is it? When stuff like that happens. It never is. I mean, I have to fire people around here, bartenders and the dancers and all. It happens. It's not easy. For anyone involved."

Actually, it had seemed easy enough for McIntyre to throw me under the bus. But I wasn't going to argue with somebody I was hoping to get a job from. "You heard I got fired?"

"I asked about you. From the people I got it from. And they told me that there'd been some kind of falling-out, between McIntyre and his head accountant. Which I figured was you. I'm really sorry about that. It seemed like you were doing a good job and all. You were able to get me off the hook with him, at least."

Taking a deep breath, I pulled myself up straight in the chair. "Then I suppose you can guess why I've come here to see you."

"I overhead you talking to my guy out front. You're looking for a job."

"That's right." I nodded. "I figured you could use a bookkeeper. A good one. Like me."

"You do, huh?"

"Well . . . you weren't too organized before. That mess with the rent payments probably wouldn't have gotten to that point, if you'd had somebody watching out for these kinds of things." I smiled as I pointed to the mess of papers on his desk. "It doesn't look like you're exactly on top of stuff now."

"You got that right." He looked at the papers in disgust. "I don't even know what half this stuff is. Running a place like this was easier, back when I took over from my old man. We did it on a cash basis then. Long as you kept your liquor supplier happy, and the cops paid off, there wasn't much else you had to worry about. Now I got IRS forms to fill out, might as well actually be in Greek for all I can make out of 'em." One of his burly hands swept across the desk. "Who comes up with all this stuff, anyway?"

"That's why you need an accountant. A bookkeeper. Somebody who can take care of everything, so you don't have to. You can just run the business, the way you like. Without being concerned about anyone coming in and shutting you down, because you didn't file the right papers on time."

"Tell me about it. I do need that. I know I do. And it's not just the feds – there's all kinds of problems I got. We're making good money here, this kind of place always does, but I'm losing track. I think one of the bouncers is raking off the door fees, and there's some punks coming around, shaking the girls down for a cut of their tips . . ." He shook his head. "That's the problem with losing track of the numbers, when you're running a business. Any kind of business. It's like blood in the water. You bleed a little and these jerks get a whiff of it, they think they can come in and rip you off even more. Gotta watch every freakin' dime these days – that's what it comes to. Just out of self-defense. Can't trust anybody anymore."

"You're right," I said. "You shouldn't have to deal with these things. I mean, with the numbers and all. I can help."

"I know you can. It's just –" He slumped down heavily in the chair behind the desk. "There's problems. Other kinds of problems."

My spine stiffened a little. "What do you mean?"

"I mean problems with hiring you. Big problems."

"Please." My facade started to crack, with my barely suppressed nervousness leaking through. "I know there are some difficulties." I thought I knew what he was talking about. "I know I don't have any kind of resume, and I don't have a lot of references. Or any." My hands knotted around each other, squeezing themselves bloodless, as I leaned toward him. "But I can do the job. You know I can –"

"That's not the problem." He sadly shook his head. "The problems aren't with you. They're with McIntyre."

"I don't . . ." His words had brought me bolt upright again. "I don't know what you mean . . ."

"It's simple, sweetheart. Too simple. I can't afford to piss the man off. I couldn't afford to do that before, and I sure as hell can't do it now." The club manager leaned back and laid his own hands across the rolling mound of his stomach. "He fired you, right? I mean, really fired you. As in your ass landing out on the street. That means there's like emotions involved, right? You know how angry McIntyre can get."

I nodded without saying anything. That was something I was more than familiar with. Especially now.

"He hears I took you on to do my books, after the way he made it clear how he feels about you, and then that gets rubbed off on me. He gets annoyed at me. More than annoyed – he gets mad. And then I'm in deep doo-doo."

"I understand." My voice dwindled down to its scared little schoolgirl whisper. "You're right."

"Try to see it from my point of view." He spread his hands apart. "I just can't afford to get on the wrong side of your old boss, not with all that's about to pop right now –"

Something clicked inside my head. Numbers, earnings projections, purchase fees, a whole scrolling column of things like that. I had seen them in the ledgers back at my old job, and on some correspondence that McIntyre had me go over for him. I looked back up at the man on the other side of the desk, my gaze narrowed and level.

"He bought you out." My voice was level now as well, coldly unemotional. "He bought this place."

"Well . . ." The manager shifted uncomfortably. "The deal's not final yet. But yeah, it's happening." A weak smile showed on his face. "It's a lot of money – I mean, by my standards. McIntyre's got a lot of plans for this place. Taking it upscale and all. Turning it into something really nice. And . . . you know . . . profitable."

"And if I'm here, keeping your books, then that's not going to happen. He'll drop the deal."

"Yeah. He'll back out. I know he will."

I wasn't looking at the manager – the owner, really – of some sleazy little strip club. That I could've kept operating in the black, just by keeping an eagle eye on the numbers. I was looking at a tired old man, who just wanted to get out. And who was scared, not so much of Mr. McIntyre, as he was of his last chance to unload the place evaporating in front of his eyes. So much for doing me a payback favor, if he ever could.

Did I tell you already, that I feel this world kind of sucks?

"I'm sorry I bothered you." I watched my own hands gathering up my purse from my lap. Then I stopped before I stood up, to give him one more chance. "He wouldn't have to know. I'd just be here in the back room. I'd stay out of sight, nobody would have to know . . ."

"I'm sorry," He looked really old then. "I just can't take the chance."

"All right." I stood up. "I understand. Believe me, I do."

"Look, uh, no hard feelings –" He called after me as I headed for the door. "Tell Ernie to set one up for you, on the house. Set up a couple. It doesn't matter if you're under-age . . ."

I couldn't hear the rest of what the manager was saying. I just kept walking until the padded rail of the bar door was against my hand. I pushed it open and stepped out into the street's eye-achingly bright sunlight.

† † †

I mulled over what I had just found out, all the way home.

A motorcycle is good for that sort of thing, as long you're not letting your emotions dictate your thoughts. You can do some cold brooding when you're leaned over the handlebars of a sportbike. Even if you shouldn't.

There had been a reason for my firing up the Ninja, out where I had left it at the curb in front of the apartment building, and using it to get around town rather than riding the bus. I had more places on my list than that one bar, to check into about getting a job. Most of them were on the less-than-seemly side, for two reasons. One, those were the kinds of places that I had learned about, and met the people who ran or owned them, while I had still being working for McIntyre. And two, with my nonexistent resume, I figured I had a better shot with those kinds of places than something respectable, a place big enough to have an HR department with interview procedures and a clipboard full of forms to fill out. The great thing about seedy places is that they're more open to paying people under the table, and I had already set my mind to cutting whatever low-ball deal I had to in order to land any kind of gig.

But now, all those plans had flown out of my head and were tumbling somewhere behind me on the road, in the dust kicked up by the motorcycle. It wasn't that the bar I'd just been to had been my best shot, with the manager having said a while back that he owed me a favor, look him up if I ever needed anything, so forth and so forth. It was the realization that I'd probably get the same reaction at every place I went into, all over the city. I knew about McIntyre's various business enterprises, every kind, from the shady to the legitimate. He had his wily little tentacles into places of every variety; I wouldn't have had to stay so late every night, going over the books, if there hadn't been so many revenue sources to track. The upshot of that being, as I realized now, that there were more people who owed McIntyre favors than would ever owe me. Or they would like to do him a favor and get something back in return from him. Let's face it, he was a good person for a businessman to be on the right side of. And if things went wrong? Not so good.

That's what McIntyre's pet thugs like Michael were useful for. There probably were plenty of business types who weren't aware that a minor employee like me had gotten the boot from McIntyre's company – why would they be? – and I might even have been able to talk my way into some kind of low-paid bookkeeper job with one of them. But at some point, and sooner rather than later, they would discover that about me, and I'd be out on the street again. Then what? Plus, I was risking the chance of bringing myself back to McIntyre's attention, when I'd just as soon stay out of his mind, completely forgotten.

So the stay put and stay out of sight strategy, of keeping it cool and finding a job – any kind of job – well, that was blown up, right in my face. In this town, I couldn't get hired at McDonald's.

I kept on thinking, as the wind streamed past my helmet.

That was a mistake. When you think, you come up with ideas. And not all of them are good.

As I wove the motorcycle through the street traffic – I was already getting pretty good at this, or so I thought – an idea settled into my brain. A plan, what to do next . . .

This one, I couldn't blame on having taken a whack to the head when I'd gone down with the bike. Something this stupid, I had to have come up with all on my own.

† † †

The only thing this plan had going for it was that I didn't have to go home to the apartment and change my clothes. I already had my business-lady outfit on.

Which was what the plan revolved around. This is what I'd been wearing a couple of days before, when I'd come waltzing into McIntyre's building, all set to start my new career as CFO of his company. Just as I expected – or at least hoped – the security guard in the lobby, the one who'd asked to see my ID card, remembered me. And waved me right on through. He hadn't seen me get thrown out in the alley, and nobody had told him about it. There were a whole batch of procedures that McIntyre and his crew would have to tighten up on, now that they were going corporate. But they hadn't yet.

Late afternoon, between three and four, there weren't that many people going in and out of the elevators. I was able to get one all to myself, heading up to the floor where I used to work.

My heart was pounding in my throat when the elevator came to a stop. All it would take would be for the doors to slide open and have McIntyre on the other side, or Michael, or any number of other people who knew that I shouldn't be there, and I'd be screwed.

Second time around, I wouldn't just be tossed out at
ground level; Michael would probably try to go for
yardage off the top of the building.

I held my breath – the elevator doors slid apart –
and nobody. I could feel my spine unclench like a boiled
ramen noodle. I stuck my head out, looked in both
directions down the hallway, and saw no one. My luck
was holding out for the moment, even if my smarts had
already departed.

Also fortunately, my cubbyhole had been over on
the other side, away from where Mr. McIntyre and the
other execs had their nicely furnished offices. I scooted
that way.

Nobody saw me going into the cramped, windowless
space where I had sweated away for so long. I breathed
a sigh of relief when I saw that my desk was still there.
If it had been moved out, it would have been Game Over
for me, at least as far as this bright idea was concerned.
I left the light off as I zipped around behind it – I knew
exactly where what I had come for would be.

I spun the dial on the bottom drawer's combination
lock – I could make out the numbers – and pulled it
open. There it was. A black vinyl binder, filled with all
the CD-ROM disks that I had burned over the last year.
Fifty-something shiny silver disks, one for each week.
My entire cumulative backup of Mr. McIntyre's
finances. All his business dealings, every dollar that
came in or went out of all the intricately entwined and
overlapping accounts, and all the funky things those
dollars did in-between. Everything. That MBA putz who
McIntyre had actually made his CFO was probably over
in his corner office right now, going through page after
page of ledgers and printouts, trying to pull all this
information together. And here it was, in the big fat

binder that I lifted out of the desk drawer with both hands.

"This the one?"

Crap. Voices at the cubbyhole doorway. I stay crouched down behind the desk so whoever it is can't see me.

"Yeah. We gotta get all this junk cleared out. Office services wants to turn it back into a broom closet. Janitors are tired of going to the basement to store their mops."

I could hear the two men clumping into the room. Holding the disk binder to my breast, I crawled under the desk. From below its edges, I could see their scuffed-up work boots on either side. The desk rose a couple of inches above my head as they grabbed it and lifted. They started carrying it toward the door, not noticing that I was scooting along underneath it.

"Hold up –"

They stopped.

"We can't get this out," continued one of them. "Not with that in the way."

I realized what he meant. One of the emptied-out file cabinets was so close to the door, they wouldn't be able to turn the desk around to get it out.

"Okay, fine." That was the other one, sounding all exasperated and put-upon. "Then let's get the other stuff out first."

"Moron. You were the one who went for this stupid desk –"

They went on bickering away as they set the desk down, its underside pressing against the back of my lowered head. I could hear them wrestling with one of the file cabinets, then dragging it out into the hallway.

I waited another minute with my breath held, until their voices faded away. I crawled out from under the desk, went to the doorway, and looked out. Nobody. I ran for the elevator.

When I got down to the lobby, I had to fight the urge to run again. With the binder under my arm, I headed for the street as nervelessly as I could . . .

† † †

I didn't call ahead to the television station. Didn't make an appointment or anything. I just went on over there, with the binder and my purse strapped to the back of the motorcycle seat behind me.

You'd think that someplace like that would be more locked down, what with all the crazy people in the world who might get ticked about something they see on a news show. Maybe it was because I looked so harmless, or like I belonged there. Most people don't seem to think that a tiny Asian girl in a business-lady suit is likely to do much damage. Maybe I've proved them wrong – but that all came later.

I left the Ninja parked out by the vans with the big transmission antennas on their roofs. Inside the building, I managed to ask around and finagle myself up to the second floor where the offices and cubicles for the various producers and reporters were. Walking around, acting as if I was supposed to be there, looking at the name plaques outside the doors, I finally found the one I was looking for.

"Can I help you?" The tall brunette pounding away at the keyboard didn't even look away from her computer screen. She radiated deadline pressure. "If it's a complaint about that zoning coverage we did on the three o'clock, you need to go talk to Dave Henderson. Wasn't my baby."

"Miss Ibanez?"

She glanced over her shoulder at me, then went back to typing. "That's right."

The name plaque outside her door actually read
KAREN IBANEZ. I had seen her a million times on the
evening news. She did a lot of reporting on local politics.
A year or so ago, she'd gotten some kind of award for a
series that had wound up getting a city councilman
bounced in a recall election. That was why I figured
she'd be the best one to talk to.

"I've got something you might be interested in." I
held the disk binder up in both hands. "Something that
might be . . . you know . . . news."

She looked at the binder, then up to my face. "So
who are you?"

I told her my name. And who I used to work for.

That got a raised eyebrow from her. "Really?"

I nodded.

"For how long?"

"A year. And a little more."

"Huh." She swiveled her chair around and leaned
back in it. "You know . . . I've had to deal with some
people before, who work for McIntyre." She folded her
arms, tilting her head to one side as she studied me. "As
a general rule, they're bigger and uglier than you are.
And they don't come around here, asking to talk to
somebody like me."

"No. They wouldn't."

"They don't even usually talk to a grand jury. Not
without a lawyer sitting on either side of them. At
least –" She gave a shrug. "The ones who are still
working for him don't. The ones who used to work for
him, they're found floating face-down in the river."

I nodded. I had cut checks, to pay for things like that
to happen.

"So how come you're standing here, still breathing
and all?"

"I don't know." I shrugged. "I guess they didn't think I was important enough to bother with. Or that I'd ever do something like this."

"That's a little hard to believe. McIntyre has a reputation for being . . . kind of thorough. About that sort of thing." She reached a hand out toward the binder. "So let me see what you got."

There was another chair in the cubicle, that I pulled over so I could sit down beside her. I opened up the binder, pulled out the most recent backup disk and fed it into her computer. A couple of pokes on her keyboard and a screenful of numbers appeared on the screen.

"Okay –" I leaned forward and jabbed a forefinger at a row of digits. "These are the transfers between one of the front companies and a couple of banks down in the Bahamas. None of this ever got reported to the currency control agencies. And this –"

I scrolled down. I was in my element now.

"This is a shuffle between a wholly owned mortgage pool and a back-end money-laundering scheme." My fingernail tapped against the screen. "You see, each one of these takes the monthly float off a union pension fund, and routing it through –"

"Yeah, yeah; right. Whatever," said the TV reporter.

The tone in her voice brought me up short.

"So is this your insurance or something?" She set back, looking at the screen. "Because you're no fool, are you? The whole time you were slaving away for McIntyre, at the back of your mind you were thinking that maybe someday he might screw you over. Right?"

"No. I don't know. Maybe."

"Sure. And that's why you kept all these records. So if something shitty happened between you and your boss, you'd be able to get back at him. Maybe blackmail him a little, huh?"

"No –" I shook my head. "That's not what I want."

"Or maybe – just get a little revenge?"

I didn't say anything.

"Doesn't matter," she said. "I don't care about people's reasons for doing things. That's not my job." She pointed to the screen. "You know what you have here?"

Shrinking back into the chair, I shook my head.

"You don't have squat. That's what you've got."

"But –"

She turned the computer screen in my direction. "On-the-Spot News brings you – numbers!" She punched a key and the screen changed. "And now – more numbers!" She punched another key and the screen went blank.

"That kind of stuff might mean a lot to you – but you're an accountant, right?" She lowered her head in order to look into my averted eyes. "You eat and breathe numbers. That's what you do. They're real to you." With her thumb, she pointed to the window across from the cubicle. "But the people out there – they could give a rat's ass. You can't even get the cops interested – you tried that already, didn't you?"

I shook my head.

"Then take my advice, and don't bother. Look, I know why you came here. Lots of people have it in for McIntyre. Including me. Yeah, I'd love to nail him. He's been the biggest dirt bag in this town for years. Nailing slime like him is what people like me do. Plus, I'd be up for a Pulitzer if I did get him. But I can't do it with junk like this."

She took the disk out of the computer and handed it back to me. I sat there looking down at it in my hands.

"Look." Her voice went softer and kinder. "Having a bunch of stuff in a computer file, or in a notebook, and somehow you can destroy somebody like McIntyre with it – that's something you see in the movies. It doesn't happen in real life."

"I guess not."

"Can I give you some more advice?"

I nodded dumbly.

"Don't get caught with this stuff on you. Get rid of it. You're in enough trouble already."

She was right. I knew that. What I didn't know, was what I had been thinking of when I had come to the television station. My first plan had fallen apart, and then just like that, I had come up with this one. Which sucked. It was all part of my head being in a bad place.

"Let me know if you come up with something else." She turned back to the computer and started typing again. "Like a videotape of McIntyre molesting a Cub Scout on the city hall lawn, with a knife held to the kid's throat. That I could use. Now if you'll excuse me . . . I've got half an hour to get down to the editing room and put together something that people actually want to watch."

I stuck the disk back into the binder, stood up, and stepped out of the cubicle.

"Hey –"

I looked back at the reporter.

"I'm sorry," she said. "You're not the only one with a grudge against McIntyre. Let's just say he hurt a lot of people on his way up." Her voice went quieter. "A lot of people."

We looked at each other for a moment longer, before I turned and walked away.

THIRTEEN

SOON AS I stepped outside the television station building, I thought I was busted.

There was a car parked alongside the motorcycle, close enough to keep me from even getting to it. And there was somebody behind the steering wheel, waiting for me.

"Hey, honey –" She had on big Hollywood-type sunglasses. Her long red hair was looped in a loose braid falling over one shoulder as she leaned out the car's window. "Come here. I want to talk to you."

I halted a couple of yards away, warily regarding her. Right now, with everything that had been going on, this couldn't be good. I wasn't in a place where good things were likely to happen.

"What do you want?"

"I told you. I just want to talk. That's all."

I didn't move, except to get out of the way of one of the news vans rolling toward the parking lot exit. "Talk about what?"

"Don't be so suspicious. I'm not going to hurt you." The woman nodded her head toward the empty passenger seat beside her. "Come on. Just get in – so we can be comfortable. Private, you know?" She flashed a big, fakey smile at me. "And we can chat. Just you and me."

I wasn't sure about that. For all I knew, there could be a half-dozen thugs crouched down in the car's back seat, ready to lay on me whatever new bad thing the world had cooked up.

Plus, my mind was racing. I had seen this woman before, but I couldn't remember where.

Then it hit me. At the club where I had gone looking for a job – she had been the woman, obviously one of the club's dancers, who had been sitting over on the stage, reading the newspaper, when I had come in. I had a vague memory of her idly glancing over at me when I had been talking to the bartender. Her hair had been all combed out loose then, a big red fall of it, just like you'd expect a dancer to have in a place like that. And flashy makeup, with eyelashes that a bird could land on. But this was the same woman.

"No –" I shook my head. No way was I getting into that car. "You can tell me whatever you want to, from here."

"Okay, you little twit. I'm not messing around." Her smile evaporated, leaving a hard, murderous look behind. "I've got stuff I want to talk to you about, and I don't want everybody in the freakin' world to hear it."

The way her words grated really had me scared. I glanced over at the lot's exit, thinking that maybe I should just run for it. I could always come back for the motorcycle later.

"Don't," warned the woman behind the steering wheel. "Just get in the car. I promise it'll be better for you if you do."

I eyed her with even more suspicion. "Why would it?"

"Oh, come on." She leaned an elbow out over the windowsill. "You used to work for McIntyre – yeah, I know all about that. And here you are, a couple of days after you got fired by him, coming out of someplace that's just stuffed with all sorts of snoopy reporters and news types." She pointed to the binder I was holding up against my breast. "I'm sure you had something interesting to show them, didn't you? You know who else would be interested? McIntyre, that's who. You don't want to talk to me, that's fine. I'll just go talk to him instead. And tell him what you were doing here. Then your skinny little butt will be cooked."

I stood there frozen, the thoughts scurrying inside my skull the only part in motion. Then I circled around to the car's passenger side, pulled open the door, and climbed in.

"Okay –" My heart pounded as I set the binder on my lap. "What do you want to talk about?"

"Cole."

"What..." I blinked at her, uncomprehending. After a couple of seconds, I was able to get a complete sentence out. "What about him?"

"You don't know?" She ran her hand across the top of the steering wheel. "You didn't hear what happened?"

"No –" I shook my head. That seemed to hook up something inside. I peered more closely at the woman. "Are you . . . Monica?"

That was the name. I was pretty sure of it. Cole had said something to me one time, back in my cubbyhole office late at night, when he had picked up one of the checks for services rendered that McIntyre had told me to cut. With that big psycho grin of his, telling me what a hot night he had lined up for himself – for him and Monica – when he got home to her. He was one of those guys who liked talking about stuff like that, especially to timid little mice like me. There was some kick involved, I suppose – not from the sex talk, but from rubbing it in that he had a life that was all sorts of exciting and wild, the kind of life that a mouse was too afraid to even think about.

The woman sitting behind the wheel was obviously her. I knew it. She not only looked like the kind of woman who would've been Cole's girlfriend, the kind of flashy creature he'd be attracted to. Not just over-amped sexually – whatever she had going on in that department, she had more of it in her little finger than I did in my entire undersized schoolgirl body – but also radiating that dangerous vibe, the certainty that people like her and Cole just didn't care what happened in this world, how much damage they caused to everyone else in it as they tore their way past us.

I had known girls like that back in the long line of high schools, none of which I'd ever had the chance to spend more than a couple of semesters in as Donnie and I had gotten shuttled from one foster home to another. Or known of, really – the way an astronomer with his eye to his telescope would know of some incredibly distant comet streaking through the sky, that he would never actually touch. Those girls scared me then, as I scurried past them to my locker, mousy head down . . .

Right now, I was terrified.

"Yeah," she said, "that's it. Cole must've said something to you about me."

"No –" I quickly shook my head. "Just . . . your name."

"Super. He told me about you."

That didn't lessen my terror. "Like what?"

"No big deal, sweetheart. Just that he got his paychecks from you. And he thought you were funny."

I managed to breathe a little bit. That wasn't too bad. It was the best that a girl like me could hope for in this world.

"So you didn't hear about what happened, huh? To Cole, I mean."

I shook my head again. "I don't know what you're talking about."

"That's cool." She nodded slowly, mulling things over to herself as she gazed out the windshield. "I wasn't sure whether you were in the loop on that or not. I should've guessed that you weren't. McIntyre probably kept you in the dark about all kinds of stuff."

"Yeah . . . you could say that."

"I just needed to make sure." She took her sunglasses off and turned her gaze toward me again. "When I saw you come into the club – you looked like the way Cole had described you."

I knew better than to ask for details about that.

"Then I checked with the manager," she said. "And he told me that you were somebody who used to work for McIntyre. So I pretty much figured it was you. Took me a little while to track you down, though. I had to ask some people."

That didn't surprise me. There were all sorts of those in the crummy neighborhood that Donnie and I lived in.

"Why . . . why did you want to find me?" I squeaked out the question. "Was it something . . . something about Cole?"

"I don't know." The expression on her high-cheekboned face darkened with brooding. "What I was going to do. If you'd had something to do with it. With what happened to him."

"I told you." My voice went all pleading. "I don't know what you're talking about."

"You really don't. Do you?" Her mouth set hard and grim. "Let's go for a drive." She reached out and turned the key in the ignition. "I'll show you."

"But –"

"Don't worry. I'll bring you back here." She dropped the car into drive and swung it around, tires squealing, toward the parking lot exit.

† † †

I don't have a lot of memories. I mean, the kind that other people do.

Donnie has more of them than I have. Even though he's younger than me. He tells me that he remembers a lot of things, from a long time ago, that I can't find anywhere inside my head. It's like an empty box that you can't throw out, even though every time you look in it, there's still nothing.

Though actually there is one thing, rattling around in that box. I try not to pick it up and look at it too often.

What it is, is a memory from when I was a little girl. I mean a little, little girl. A child. Donnie must've been just a baby then, so how can he remember any of these things? But here's what I remember. It's not much. Somebody's leading me by the hand – I don't know who it is and I can't see the person's face; I'm so little that I barely seem to come up past their knee. It's a long white corridor, and it smells funny, like bleach, only it's not bleach, and there are lots of doors with numbers on them. And past the doors are funny-looking beds, complicated-looking ones, with different kinds of machines around them, with hoses and tubes and wires coming out of them, and a little television screen with nothing but a green line ticking up and down across it. There are people in those funny beds, but from down where I am, I can't see their faces. But I can hear their slow, labored breathing, in time to the chugging and clicking of the machines.

There's not much more. Whoever it is that has me by the hand, we finally reach the room at the end of the hallway. And we go into one of the rooms, crowded with the funny bed and all the other stuff. And whoever it is lets go of my hand and picks me up around my waist, then lifts me so I can see the person in the bed.

I don't remember the next part. I just remember all the funny machines going silent, and the room seeming to get much bigger all around me. While the green line on the little TV screen stopped hiccupping up and down, and just went flat . . .

That's why I hate hospitals.

Probably why most people do. Stuff like that.

So I have to figure that Cole's girlfriend Monica was just being sadistic by bringing me there. She could've just told me and my head would've been messed up enough, just by knowing. But she wanted to see my reaction. See it in my face. Things weren't going the way she wanted them to, either – so somebody had to pay. Even just a little bit. I just happened to be the one she glommed on to.

The corridor Monica led me down had that same disinfectant smell that I remembered. The room wasn't at the end of the hallway, though; it was about halfway down. Close to the nurses' station. In the intensive care ward, there were a lot more machines hooked up inside the rooms.

One of the nurses, with a clipboard in her hands, was inspecting the bags of fluids hanging up like sad, soft Christmas ornaments all around one of the beds. Narrow tubes ran from the bottoms of the slowly collapsing bags to the figure lying motionless in the bed, with the sheet drawn up across his chest. The nurse gave a little nod of recognition to Monica, then slipped out to make room for us.

I gripped the bed's raised chrome rail with both hands as I leaned over and looked down at Cole. Even with there being so little of his face exposed, with the big ridged air hose locked into his mouth and the other hoses threaded down his nose, with the surgical tape holding everything in place, including all the wires and patches monitoring his vital signs – even with all that, I knew it was him. I knew it was him as soon as we stepped into the room.

It's a strange thing looking at somebody in the hospital, somebody really messed up like that – when it's somebody you've always been afraid of.

I wasn't afraid of Cole now. I just felt sorry for him.

And sorry, and scared, for myself. Because if something like this could happen to him – whatever it had been – then anything could happen. To anyone, including me and Donnie. Cole had been the scariest person in the world. To see him lying there, his eyes closed, nothing moving except his chest rising and falling in time to the respirator clacking away beside the bed . . .

I turned and looked over my shoulder at Monica. "What happened?"

"What do you think?" Her voice was tight and bitter, her eyes two narrowed slits. "Same as what happened to you."

I nodded, silent.

"He got fired," said Monica.

† † †

She had lied to me. She didn't drive me back over to the television station. She stayed there at the hospital, beside Cole's bed.

I walked back. Carrying the black binder in both arms across my breast. It started to rain before I had gone more than a few blocks, but I didn't mind. That way, nobody could tell if I was crying or not.

Even when I got to the TV station, unstrapped my helmet from the back of the seat, and pulled it on. I left the visor up as I rode through the glistening wet streets. Hoping that the wind and the rain would just wash everything away . . .

PART TWO

Enough bad shit happens without trying.
Your job is to make sure it happens to the
right people.
　　　　　 – Cole's Book of Wisdom

FOURTEEN

AFTER THAT, at least for a few days, I didn't care what happened. If any of the lowlifes slinking around the apartment building figured out that Donnie and I were getting by on that money I had sorta, kinda stolen from McIntyre – I just didn't care.

I should've spent the time thinking about what I was going to do next, but I didn't. It's not like I was having any great success coming up with plans. I'd already had, in short order, two of them come crashing apart. The bit about keeping my head low and going out and getting a job, any kind of job, so that nobody would suspect that I might be hanging onto something that wasn't mine and was McIntyre's instead – that had gone right out the window. And then the crazier plan that had popped into my head right after that, about going to the television station with the binder full of backup disks, and just bringing his whole evil empire down with all those financial records – what a joke. The news reporter had been kind to me when she had filled me in on the nature of reality, that doing things like that wasn't part of it.

Given that track record, I wasn't even sure I should try coming up with another plan. Yeah, I know the third time's the charm and all, but what exactly was that supposed to mean? Maybe I'd come up with something that worked and solved all our problems for us – or maybe it meant the next one would wind up getting both of us killed.

Or maybe we'd get killed, no matter what I did. Or if I did nothing at all. I didn't know.

That's another problem with being in a bad place. There are no exits. Every door either leads to something worse, or back to where you were.

So a couple of weeks went by that way, with me staring out the window, down to the street below, and Donnie knowing better than to bug me.

I took a couple of nibbles out of the money from the envelope – I had to. First to pay the rent, then to get some more groceries into the place. It turned out that in this neighborhood, breaking a hundred-dollar bill at the corner market didn't draw as much attention as I had been concerned that it would. I figured it out; it was because of the hookers. The grizzled old guy behind the cash register just gave me my change and a look of respect I'd never gotten before. As though I had finally figured out a way of making more money than I had at my crappy accountant job, though who he figured I was peddling it to, other than guys who were into twelve-year-old boys, was beyond me.

Another week goes by, and I still don't have a clue. If it hadn't been for the money in the envelope – I still kept it hidden on the closet shelf, under the sweaters – I suppose my brother and I would've just sat inside the apartment and starved to death. Too scared to leave town, too freaked to come up with another plan. Unless waiting for some other bad thing to happen constitutes a plan.

"Hey! Kim!" A shout came at me as I was coming back from another run to the store. "Come over here – I want to talk to you."

With my arms full of the grocery bags, I looked over and saw a car that I had ridden in before, pacing me.

Monica was steering with one hand while leaning toward the rolled-down window on the passenger side.

"We talked before." I kept walking. "I didn't enjoy it."

"Yeah, well, I can understand you feeling that way." Monica kept cruising alongside me. "Think it was fun for me?"

"Fun for you?" I stopped and stared at her. "It was your idea! I didn't want to go to that stupid hospital. And see . . ." I let my words drift away unspoken.

"Okay, okay." She had stopped the car as well. "Forget what I said. I don't want to talk to you."

"Great." I lifted the bags higher in my arms and started walking again. "Thanks for dropping by."

Usually I wasn't so sarcastic with people. Even the ones I couldn't stand. I guess holing up in our crappy little apartment, slowly going nuts, had started to give me a little bit of an edge.

"There's someone else who wants to talk to you –"

I stopped and looked back at her in the car. "Yeah? Who?"

"It's Cole."

That gave me something to think about. Even if I couldn't.

"Well . . ." I looked down inside the bags, then up at her again. "I can't go with you right now. I've got ice cream here. I don't want it to melt."

"Look. I'll buy you more ice cream. Just get in the car."

I got into the car – I'm not sure why. Maybe I was the one who wanted to talk to somebody.

† † †

After a few blocks, I realized Monica wasn't driving toward the hospital.

"Where are we going?"

"Home," she said. "Our home. I mean where Cole and I live."

"Oh." I looked at the buildings going by. "So he's not at the hospital? Not any more?"

"Duh. They let him go home."

"Wow. That's great. So he's all recovered and stuff?"

"I said he went home." She didn't look over at me. "Let's leave it at that."

When we got close to the wharves, I could smell the oil-stained river water. There were warehouses and loading docks all around us, when Monica pulled the car over to a stop.

"We're here." She pushed her door open. "Come on."

She led me to the small, normal-sized door at the side of one of the warehouses. A lop-eared dog barked at us from the other side of a rattling chain-link fence. Beer cans and a few syringes were scattered in the dry, trodden-down weeds between the stretches of broken concrete.

I'd never been in a warehouse before, at least not that I could remember. This one was a big, mostly empty space, with just a few ancient cardboard cartons with Chinese lettering on them, stacked up by the loading dock door. The rafters were streaked with white droppings from the pigeons that fluttered up near the ceiling. Dusty sunlight filtered in through the high, broken windows.

"Over here." Monica headed toward the rear of the warehouse.

The two of them had made a little home for themselves, in a walled-off section of the building. That is, if you think of home as any place with a mattress on the floor and a lot of guns.

There had probably been more of them at one time – the guns, I mean – judging by the dirty silhouettes on the walls. Guns and other things, the stuff Cole had used to do his job with.

"Yo – I'm back."

No answer came from the figure lying curled up under a blanket on the dirty mattress.

Monica went over and prodded the lumpy shape with the toe of her boot. "Wake up," she said. "We got company." She looked over at me. "Come here and say hello to the man of the house."

The figure stirred and rolled onto one shoulder. I could barely recognize him. His face was all bony and gaunt, the stubble matching the gray buzz-cut that his shock of yellow hair had been shaved down to.

"Gotta take a leak," mumbled Cole. He didn't open his eyes. "I mean like now."

"Least you held it 'til I got home." Monica gazed down at him, her own face set hard and expressionless. "Not like last time." Over to me again. "Don't you want to say hello?"

I stepped over to the edge of the mattress. Even the blue of his eyes seemed faded and washed out as he rolled the back of his head on the thin pillow and looked up at me.

"Hey . . ." Cole managed a woozy smile. "It's our little accountant. The girl with the adding machine. And the checkbook." He propped himself up on one skinny elbow. "Didja bring me a check?"

"No." I shook my head. "I don't have one for you. Not today."

"Too bad. Coulda used it." He rolled farther onto his side and rummaged in a plastic bucket for a bottle of pills. He downed a couple of them with a swallow of grocery-store vodka. "Stuff costs, ya know."

"Yes . . . I know."

"Hope you'll 'scuse me if I don't stand up and shake your hand. Got a problem doing that, these days. Standing up, I mean."

He rooted around some more in the litter around the mattress, coming up at last with a half-empty pack of cigarettes. "Hey, honey – where's my lighter?"

"Here you go." Monica squatted down on her haunches and lit the cigarette for him. "How's that?"

"Righteous." He took a deep drag, then coughed hard enough to shake his entire body, the blanket falling away from his bare chest. "That's the best." The cigarette hung off his lower lip as he dug the points of his elbows into the mattress. He dragged himself into a sitting position against the wall behind him, his legs dragging limply along under the blanket. "The absolute . . . freakin' best."

I couldn't say anything more. This was worse than the hospital.

"Glad you could come by." He coughed some more, than wiped his mouth with the back of his hand. "Nice to see people. You know . . . like for old times' sake." His crooked smile lifted a corner of his mouth. "There haven't been a lot of 'em. Matter of fact, you're the only one. Who's come to see me –" Another coughing spell racked his frame. "Ain't that crazy?" He shook his head. "Makes ya wonder what they're afraid of. I mean – you're not afraid of me, are you? Not any more, that is."

"No . . ." What I felt was worse.

"So it's nice. Ya know? Because . . . I don't get out much anymore." His barking laugh turned into another cough that doubled him over, ash from the cigarette falling across the blanket over his lap. He used his free hand to push himself back up. "Just the way it is, sweetie."

"Monica said . . . you wanted to see me."

"I did?" He looked over at her. "Did I tell you that?"

"Yeah," she said. "You did. That's why I went over and got her. And brought her here."

"Huh. Imagine that." He scratched the side of his head. "That's really . . . strange. Because that's not what I think is going on."

His dark-circled gaze locked onto mine.

"It's what you wanted. Isn't it, Kim? You wanted to come and see your old pal. Didn't you?"

" I don't know . . . what you mean . . ."

Cole suddenly lunged forward, one hand grabbing my ankle. Squeezing tight.

"That was nice of you." His face split with his crazy grin. "To want to come and see me. You remember – good times, huh? But there's something more. Isn't there?"

I couldn't pull myself free. I almost stumbled and fell backward as I struggled against his grasp.

"Isn't there?"

And then I knew he was right. When Monica had shown up in the car, when I had been walking home from the store – part of me hadn't been surprised at all. For part of me, it had been like an answered prayer. That I hadn't even heard myself whispering.

"I . . ."

"You what? What is it, Kim?" His knuckles whitened. "It's not what I wanted. It's what you wanted. What is it? Just to say hello? That's so nice of you. Really nice. Is that all you wanted? Is it?"

Everything around me blurred as tears filled my eyes. Now I was scared.

"I thought . . ."

"Thought what? Thought what?"

"I don't know . . . I don't know . . ."

He let go of me, so suddenly that it staggered me backward.

"Did you get what you wanted? Is this what you wanted to see? Huh? Is it?"

I turned and ran. Catching myself against the doorway, I could see Cole looking down at himself and the wet stain seeping through the blanket over his crotch. "Aw, crap," he muttered.

It was dark outside when I stumbled out of the warehouse. A long walk home, and I didn't know the way.

† † †

Donnie had stayed up for me. In his wheelchair, in the middle of the front room, the lights off.

"You were gone a long time," he said.

"I know." I sat down at the table. I laid my hands flat on top of it. "The ice cream," I said after a moment. "I forgot the ice cream."

FIFTEEN

I DIDN'T know it at the time – but there were really other bad things going on. It was probably just as well that I didn't know, given how screwed up my head was then.

Those bad things were happening back at the office building where I used to work. At McIntyre's company. Since I wasn't there, watching and listening like a fly on the wall, I can't tell you exactly what happened. But I figure it went something like this –

Michael, the thuggy security guy, comes into McIntyre's office, like a garbage scow parking itself at a landfill dock. McIntyre is going over some reports that his new pet MBA, the one who got the CFO position, routed over to him. He doesn't look up from them as Michael lumbers to a halt.

"Sit down."

Michael squeezes his bulk into the chair in front of the desk.

"Okay . . ." McIntyre makes some pen marks on one of the columns of numbers. "So what is it you wanted to talk to me about?"

"Security," says Michael.

"Well, that's your job, isn't it?" More little marks.

"That's why I wanted to talk to you. I think we got some problems. Security problems."

"Really?" McIntyre lays his pen down and leans back in his office chair. "Such as?"

"Cole."

That gets a raised eyebrow. "What about him?"

"I don't think it was such a good idea to just dump him. And not take care of him. I mean, permanently take care of him."

"Oh? Why?"

"He's dangerous," says Michael.

"Dangerous?" McIntyre smiles. "He can't even walk. That's why I pulled strings down at the District Attorney's office and got the charges against him dropped. If I were worried about him, I would've let him wind up in some prison hospital."

"Yeah, but –"

"Seriously," says McIntyre. "If my head security guy is afraid of a cripple, then maybe I need to get a new one."

"Wait a minute – I'm not scared of Cole –"

"Okay, fine, you're not." McIntyre puts his fingertips together in front of himself. "But if you're bitching about him being alive instead of dead – exactly whose fault is that? You're the one who put together that set-up on him."

"It should've killed him," glowers Michael. "Phony bastard."

"Guess he's a little tougher than you anticipated. You should've known that just a shotgun wasn't enough to kill him."

All ugly and stewing, Michael doesn't say anything.

"Besides – what does it matter?" McIntyre picks up the report again. "He's sidelined. A severed spinal column tends to do that." McIntyre studies the numbers for a few seconds, then looks over the top of the printout. "You still here?"

"I just don't like it," says Michael. "You should let me take care of him."

"I thought you did."

"Permanently, I mean."

McIntyre shakes his head. "We're not that kind of a business anymore. We just don't go around killing people. Or if we do, we need a good reason."

"I think we do," says Michael. "We need to finish the job."

"You know what I think?" McIntyre lays the report down again. "I think you need to learn some modern management principles. When somebody is removed from an organization, it's no good to keep on fretting about them. They are just . . . gone."

Michael slouches down in the chair, his expression heavy and brooding.

"It's a waste of time to worry about them. They no longer exist. Understand?"

McIntyre dismisses Michael with a wave of his hand.

"You want to worry about things that don't exist, go ahead. I'm too busy."

Michael simmers for a moment longer, then gets up and leaves the office.

† † †

As I said, something like that probably went down between the two of them. The day after I had found out that Cole was still alive, that he hadn't died in the hospital where I had seen him, I could picture the whole exchange inside my head. A mixture of good and bad: if McIntyre, in his lofty superior way, couldn't be bothered with the people he had thrown to the curb, the ones who didn't fit into his new corporate business model, then that was good for me. It meant that I didn't exist for him anymore. Which was right here where I wanted to be – at least as long as nobody figured out what my younger brother and I were living on, the envelope full of money stashed in the bedroom closet. So maybe we had a little breathing room. When enough time had passed, maybe

Donnie and I could sneak out of town, just disappear, with nobody thinking anything of it, nobody making a connection. Maybe.

The bad, of course, was that the longer we waited, the more chance there could be that it could all unravel – and the two of us would still be here, like sitting ducks. Maybe there already was somebody who'd figured it out, that the reason I could flash a $100 bill at the corner store wasn't because I had put together a lucrative new career in renting my tush out to some clientele who liked 'em lightweight. But because I had done some sticky-fingered number on my former employer. Who wouldn't be happy to hear about it, and for whom I would then exist again, though not for long.

That, plus the Michael thing. He might not be sulking about me still being alive, but I'd had enough run-ins with him while we both had still been working for the same boss, that I knew how his berserker Neanderthal mind worked. For a guy like that, the only way to get somebody he disliked out of his mind was to kill the person. For somebody like Michael, there was only one kind of dead.

And somebody might've seen me with Cole's girlfriend Monica. Out on the street, or at the hospital, or over at that warehouse dump where they lived, out by the wharves. And then told Michael about it. So there would be a connection in his rat-like brain between me and Cole. That was definitely not good. I knew he'd go on sulking about Cole, until he figured out exactly what he wanted to do about him, that he might finally be able to convince his boss McIntyre to go along with. Whatever the plans were that Michael might come up with, I didn't want to be part of them.

So those were the kinds of things that I was brooding about, as I sat at the little table in the apartment kitchenette. Looking out the window and not seeing the crappy, trash-strewn street down below, but instead all the bad movies that were playing on the screen behind my eyes . . .

Until I finally came to a decision. A plan of my own.

I went into the bedroom. "I'm going out," I told Donnie. I was already pulling on my jacket – not the one from the business-lady outfit, but the cheap leather one I'd picked up, for when I was riding the motorcycle. Even when the sun was out. If I went down again, better the jacket should take the scrape rather than my precious skin.

He looked up at me. "Where to?"

"Don't worry." I leaned over and kissed him on the forehead. "I'll be back before you know it."

I headed for the apartment's front door. Actually, I didn't know if I would be back at all.

It was that kind of a plan.

† † †

A little while later, I was slowing the Ninja down and coming to a stop outside Cole's warehouse abode. I didn't see Monica's car parked anywhere nearby. Maybe she was out working, at the club where I'd first spotted her or somewhere else just like it. That suited me fine.

I left the motorcycle at the curb and went around to the door on the side of the building. As I'd expected would be the case, it was unlocked. Anybody who had a notion of ripping Cole off, while he was sitting there in the middle of his lethal toys, would've first been an idiot, then a corpse.

That was why I called out to him, soon as I slipped inside. I didn't want him letting off a shot at me.

"Hey, Cole –" My voice echoing in the empty space sent a couple of roosting pigeons into a flutter near the ceiling. "You're here, aren't you?"

"Where the hell else would I be?" His voice came from the walled-off section beyond. "Sounds like my little friend Kim. Come on back."

This time, he had on a T-shirt, a ratty-looking black number with an NRA emblem printed on it. He was still sitting on the mattress, adding one cigarette butt after another to the overfilled ashtray beside it, and watching a portable TV set up on a folding chair.

"This or The View." With his cigarette, he pointed to the cartoons bouncing around on the TV screen. "And I hate those broads." He picked up a remote from on top of the blanket and switched off the set. "Find yourself something to sit on. Make yourself comfortable."

There was another chair at a wobbly card table, covered with empty Chinese food cartons, at the side of the space. I dragged it over to the foot of the mattress and sat down.

"So." He took a lung-filling drag from the cigarette. "Nice of you to come by again. On your own steam."

I glanced around to make sure we were by ourselves. "Monica's not here?"

"Come on. You know that." He exhaled a gray cloud. "You wouldn't have come in if she were." He leaned back, regarding me with his ice-blue eyes. "She's out working. Somebody's got to cover the weekly nut. I'm not exactly the breadwinner for our little family anymore."

"She's . . . a hard worker." I sat there with my hands in my lap, not knowing what else to say. "The day after . . ."

"The day after I got shot?" That amused him. "Just say it, sweetie. Not like I don't know what you're talking about."

I nodded. "The day after . . . I saw her at one of the clubs. Where I guess she works."

"Yeah, I know all about that. She told me – about seeing you." He lit another cigarette from the butt of the previous one. "That's where she would've been, all right. Out there, getting ready to hustle for the tips. She probably seemed all calm and collected, didn't she?"

Another nod. "Kind of."

"A lot of people think she's sort of a cold piece. But that's just the way she is. If she was holding it together, that was because she knew somebody was going to have to take care of business, after I got out of the hospital. The doctors had already told her what kind of shape I was going to be in, if I pulled through. Anyway, screw all that." He peered more closely at me through the haze of smoke. "How are you doing? That's a more important question."

"I'm fine," I said. "Getting by."

"That's great. That's really great." He tilted his head back, to blow the next cloud up toward the warehouse ceiling. "Everybody's doing just . . . great. Aren't we? All things considered."

I kept silent, one hand squeezing the other in my lap.

"You know . . . I had a feeling that you were going to come around here again." Cole gave a slow nod, watching me. "I can usually tell what people are going to do. Very handy in my former line of work."

"Sure," I said. "I imagine so."

"Including what people are going to say. What they're going to ask me." His gaze followed the drifting smoke he'd exhaled, before swinging toward me again. "What you're going to ask me."

"Okay . . ." My heart was speeding up. "You know . . ."

"Yeah," said Cole. "I know why you came here to see me. I just want to hear you say it." He leaned his head back against the wall, smiling. "Just say it. All you got to do."

If I said it . . . it would be real. It wouldn't be just inside my head anymore.

And then I'd have to deal with it. Instead of just think about it.

Maybe this one I will blame on the motorcycle accident, on taking the whack to the skull. Maybe things did get screwed up in there. I still had moments when I could look out the dirty apartment window and see everything go flat and insubstantial, all the shapes in the streets painted on transparent plastic, one layer laid over another.

And I could still see – or just kind of feel – things peering out from beneath those sheets. Watching me.

Waiting for me.

"Okay." I took a deep breath, my narrow shoulders rising, then let it out. "I want to hire you."

"Hire me?" That got a laugh from him. "To do what?"

"Kill McIntyre."

There had been a time, not too long ago, when somebody like me wouldn't have said something like that. That somebody I had been before.

Cole's gaze filled with a crazy sort of excitement.

"Okay," he said.

† † †

Then he sent me out for a pizza.

And coffee. He said he didn't like to discuss business on an empty stomach. And that he liked being a little more caffeinated than his girlfriend Monica had been keeping him.

When I was on the motorcycle, heading for the place he'd given me directions to – out at the foot of one of the wharves, some longshoreman place that'd been there forever – another idea popped into my head. A better one.

Namely, that I should just forget about the pizza – I wasn't exactly capable of eating right now – and wheel the bike around in a U-turn, point it away from the warehouse district, and just head on home. And forget about what I'd just told Cole. About what I wanted to do. Hire him and all that.

Instead, I headed on over to the pizza place by the wharf. Just rolling on the accelerator and leaning over the gas tank.

Because, here's my own personal piece of wisdom: This didn't come from Cole. I figured it out on my own.

Once you decide to have somebody killed, you might as well. Because you're already screwed up, to have gotten to that point.

I didn't relate this genius insight to Cole, when I got back to the warehouse. I just sat and watched him scarf down the pizza – heavy on the meat; what did you expect – as I picked at the oily mushrooms on the one slice I'd taken. I could feel its orange-colored grease soaking through the paper plate on my lap, and into my jeans.

"That was okay." Cole set the flat white box aside, with the crescents of gnawed-on crusts in it. "Next time, if you ask for them, they'll put anchovies on. But you gotta ask. Most people don't go for 'em."

"That's because they're disgusting." I was starting to feel a little sulky. I had started a clock ticking inside my head and here we were instead, talking about pizza. "They're slime."

"Huh. That's weird. I would've thought that'd be something you'd like. Sorta like sushi."

"That's Japanese. I'm Korean. At least my parents were." I was pretty sure they'd both been born in Los Angeles, but that really didn't make any difference.

"So there's no Korean sushi?"

"How the hell would I know?"

Now I was getting pissed. When you've put killing somebody on the agenda, just about everything else seems like wasting time.

"That's good," said Cole, nodding. "That you got a temper. You didn't use to. You didn't have squat. And you're going to need something along those lines, for what you want to get done." He opened up a fresh pack of cigarettes – I'd picked that up for him, too – and lit one. "So let's talk. Business, I mean."

"Finally."

"So you want to have McIntyre iced." Another cloud of smoke drifted up toward the rafters. "Don't get me wrong, but . . . more I think about it . . . that seems a little extreme. Know what I mean?"

"How do you figure?" His words puzzled me. "It's the sort of thing you used to do all the time."

"I'm not talking about me. I'm talking about you. How old are you?"

"What is this, an interview? I thought I was the one doing the hiring."

"I don't get out a lot," said Cole. "Not anymore. So I have to maximize these little social opportunities."

"Okay, but this is business. I was expecting it to be more straightforward."

"We'll get there." He flicked ash onto the blanket. "I just need to know a little more about where your head's at. Because let's face it, you're not exactly my typical client. That's why I asked how old you are."

I told him.

"Yeah . . ." He nodded. "You can't even go into a bar and order a drink. Not legally. And now you want to hire a hit man. Even a dinged-up one like me. That's what I meant when I said extreme."

"I couldn't hire you legally, no matter how old I am. Not to do something like this. So what's the difference?"

"The difference is that most little things like you, something upsets them, they go to the mall. Buy themselves a new pair of shoes or something. They might chit-chat with their friends about wanting to have somebody killed, but they don't actually go ahead and make arrangements for it."

"I don't have a lot of friends." Any, actually; that was how far down I'd had my head in McIntyre's account books. "So that option's off the table."

"If you say so." Cole took another long drag off his cigarette. "But even if you're all bloodthirsty right now – how do I know you're going to stay that way? More likely you'll get over yourself, find something else to do besides have people killed. You move on, I'm stuck halfway through this little project – and then how do I get paid for the work I've done? Go to small claims court and ask for my money?"

"I'm not going to change my mind."

"All right. Let's say you're just as hard as you claim to be. Still a little concerned about how you suddenly got this way. Because having somebody killed isn't the first thing that pops into most people's heads. And especially not yours."

"It wasn't suddenly." I'd already thought about how I'd gotten to this point. "It makes sense. I've already paid for people to get killed. That's what I did when I was working for McIntyre. I knew what he was paying you to do. And I got used to it. It took a while, but I did. Because I didn't have a choice. That was my job, to write the checks for you. The only difference now is that I wouldn't be doing it for McIntyre. I'd be doing it for me. What I wanted to have done."

"Got a point, I suppose." He mulled it over a bit. "And can't say as I blame you. But it's kind of a join-the-club thing, if you get my meaning. There's a lot of people who'd like to have him get offed. For all kinds of reasons. Yet somehow . . ." A slow, meditative nod. "Somehow he's still walking around. Why do you suppose that is, Kim?"

"I don't know." I shrugged. "Because he's all protected and stuff, I suppose. He's got security guys, like Michael and the others. Bodyguards. That kind of thing."

"Well, you're wrong about that." Cole fished a crust out of the pizza box and took a bite from one end. Talking about killing people seemed to have stimulated his appetite. "That's not the reason. The problem isn't what McIntyre's got. It's what other people don't have. You know what that is?"

"No. But I have a feeling you're going to tell me."

"Good, good; keep that up. Because that's what those other people, the ones who'd like to see McIntyre dead, that's what they're lacking. That's guts." From under the blanket, he pulled out a huge black pistol – his favorite .357, I found out later – cocked it and pointed it straight at my face. "Because I think you know that I could cook one between your eyes right now, for sassin' me, and I couldn't even be bothered to blink about it. Nothing going to happen to me, worse than what already has."

I held my breath and sat real still. Looking down a gun barrel, so close that it seems big as a garage door, will make most people do that.

"So I don't know," he continued. "What exactly you were considering. What your plans are." He laid the gun down on the blanket and took another bite of pizza crust. "I mean – did you want to hire a hall or something, big meeting space, get everybody there who's got a grudge against your old boss. Maybe do a little networking. Like somehow that's going to get the job done."

"You don't seem to have heard me right." Without somebody pointing a gun at my head, I was all kinds of brave. "When I told you what I wanted. I don't care who else wants McIntyre killed. I just want him dead. For my own reasons. That's why I'm talking to you."

"Oh, yeah; you did say something like that." He faked being impressed with another nod. "Bloodthirsty little thing, aren't you? You got any idea about how I'm supposed to pull that off? I'm not exactly in the best of shape right now."

"Well . . ." I had thought about it. Just not a lot. "I guess . . . I could help you."

"Sure." He nodded. "You could be a lot of help on a job like this. You could bring along your adding machine and keep track of all the shots I fire. You know – just so we'd have a record and stuff."

"You don't have to be sarcastic. Just tell me if you'll do it or not."

"Take on your little job? Why should I?"

"I told you. I'm hiring you. That means I'd pay you."

"Not enough," he said, "to make it worth my while. I'm kinda retired, if you know what I mean. Like I said – the girlfriend's taking care of the bills now. And maybe I enjoy still being alive, rather than getting the rest of my ass shot off by Michael and those other bodyguards you mentioned. So . . ." He tilted his head to one side, watching me. "You'd need to come up with some other reason."

"All right." I looked straight back at him. "How's this? You'd do it – because you want him dead, too. After what he did to you."

"Not bad." Cole gave another nod. "Let's say that's true. Because it is." He pointed toward the far end of the warehouse, where the door was. "But you'd be better off just walking out of here and taking care of McIntyre yourself. Instead of wasting your money on some cripple. Whaddaya think I'm going to do, crawl downtown with my gun in my teeth and plug him one?"

"I . . . don't know . . ." Whatever I'd been thinking, it hadn't gotten that far.

"Tell you what. Why don't you just go and do it? He's not that hard to get to. You know his address – at least where he works. Head on over there. Here, you can borrow this." He picked the gun up by its barrel and held it out to me. "Think I'm going to stop you? Even if I could?"

Part of me wanted to take the gun out of his hand. And point it at him and pull the trigger.

"Because you're right," said Cole. "Think you got some big grievance against McIntyre?" The crazy smile was long gone now, replaced by something uglier. "Sonuvabitch threw me away like a used Kleenex. I worked for him longer than you did, sweetheart –" He jabbed the gun butt toward me. "And I did more for him, more dirty work, the kind where I could've gotten blown away any time. It wasn't you and your pocket calculator that put him on top – it was me."

"I know how you feel," I said quietly.

"You do, huh? The hell you do. When you got fired, it left you still walking around. Meanwhile, I'm lying here in my own mess half the time, waiting for my girlfriend to come home and wipe me, after ten hours of showing off her rack to every moron with the price of a beer."

"Okay." I tried to keep my own voice calm and level. "You know that McIntyre bought that club, don't you? The one where I met Monica the first time –"

"Of course I know. That's how she got the job. It's the only place that'd hire her. She's a little up there, to be competing with the nineteen-year-olds, if you know what I mean." Cole laughed, except that it wasn't a laugh. "And McIntyre knows she's hooked up with me. But he likes her working there. While I'm here, like this. That's just the kind of guy he is. I've heard him talk a big line about how when he gets rid of somebody, they just don't exist for him. Lemme tell ya, that's crap. He digs on it. That's the kind of sick bastard he is. He gets a kick out of something like this."

"Maybe," I said. "Maybe he cares that way about you. But he doesn't about me." That was what was so galling. "I don't exist for him. Not any more. If I ever did."

"Count your blessings." Cole set the gun down again, but his hand stayed on it as he looked sullenly away.

"No –"

He glanced over at me, watching from the corner of his eye.

"I'd like it better if he did care enough to screw with me." I hadn't figured all of this out before, at least not in words, but it had all become clear now. "That'd be better. Than not being anything at all."

Something showed in Cole's gaze. Almost like . . . respect.

"That's why I want you to kill McIntyre." I leaned forward, bringing my face down close to his. "And I'll help you do it. Whatever it takes."

Cole shrugged. "What's that supposed to mean?"

"You tell me."

This time, it was Cole who stayed silent. Looking at me.

"You're serious," he said after a couple of seconds had ticked by. "You actually mean it."

"I don't have a choice. I'm in kind of a jam –"

I told him about the money. In the envelope, stashed in the bedroom closet back at my apartment. And how it had gotten there.

When I was done, Cole gave a slow nod. "You're right," he said. "When McIntyre finds out – and he will – then you're cooked."

"I know." I also knew that it wouldn't be just me. It'd be me and whoever else was there when the bad stuff started to happen. It'd be my brother, too. There wouldn't be any loose ends left behind.

"So . . ." Cole mulled it over. "This little business proposition of yours . . ."

"I'll pay you." It was all I could think of to say. "Whatever you want."

"Don't sweat it." He waved me off. "I'm thinking about it."

"What's there to think about? Are you going to do it or not?"

"Don't rush me. I got other business to take care of."

He was driving me nuts. "Like what?"

Cole pulled the blanket off his useless legs. "I gotta take a dump." His gaze turned sly as he looked up at me. "Partner."

We were on.

I reached down and managed to get him upright, with his weight slung across my shoulders.

"It's over there." He nodded toward another, smaller door at the corner of the walled-off space. "The plumbing, I mean."

We started making our way over to it.

"You know," said Cole. "It's not going to be pretty."

"What?" I dragged him along. "You killing McIntyre?"

"That, too."

SIXTEEN

"YOU'RE UP to something. Aren't you?"

I was making a pot of tea in the apartment kitchenette. I looked over my shoulder and saw that Donnie had rolled in from his bedroom.

"What do you mean?"

"Come on, Kimmie." He gave me an accusing look. "You've been lying on the couch until 2 p.m., most days, just staring up at the ceiling. Or going two or three days without taking a shower. And now you're up early, and you're all dressed, 'stead of in your bathrobe. So you must be going somewhere. So you're up to something."

"Gosh." I poured two cups, one for him and one for me. "I didn't know there was a detective in the house."

"It doesn't take much." He held his in both hands. "I've known you all my life."

"Okay. So you're so smart – what do you think it is? That I'm up to."

"You got a job." He took a sip of his coffee. "Somebody must've called you back. From before, when you were going out looking."

I had never lied to him before.

"You're right," I said. "I've got a job."

I wasn't lying.

† † †

More coffee. Cheap store-brand instant this time, out of the cardboard box that Monica kept their groceries in. Mostly microwave soup packets and instant oatmeal. I'd had to wait outside the warehouse, with

134

both myself and the motorcycle out of sight, until Monica had driven away to whatever exotic-dancer gig she'd lined up for the day.

"Okay . . ." I watched Cole ladle a diabetic coma-inducing amount of sugar into the cup I'd made him, using just the hot water tap in the warehouse's funky little bathroom. We were both taking it black, since I'd knocked the jar of creamer into the toilet. "So let's say I go ahead and off McIntyre for you." He took a sip of the tepid coffee, then added more sugar. "What do I get out of it?"

"I thought we went over this already."

"Let's go over it again. Just to make sure we're on the same page."

"Okay. Whatever. For one thing, I'm paying you –"

"Besides that."

"And you'd get the same thing I'd get out of it." I drank a little from my cup. The last time I'd had coffee like this, I'd been a little kid living with a foster family somewhere in Oklahoma. Whoever made the stuff, they'd improved it since then. "That's what."

"Which is?"

"He'd be dead." I set my cup down on the other cardboard box – it'd held ammo before – that we were using for a table, over by the mattress on the floor. "Isn't that enough?"

"Yeah, for you maybe."

I had already told him about my previous plans going bust. On top of what I'd told him about the money-stuffed envelope hidden in the bedroom closet. Full disclosure and all – I figured that if we were going to have a shot at pulling this off, I couldn't be keeping stuff like that from him.

"You get a lot more than I do," said Cole. "You get let off the hook. Right now, you're sweating it because you've got something that belongs to him, and when he finds out that you do, he's going to come down on you like a fifty-pound sledgehammer. Michael and one of the other company security guys – there's a bullet-head named Louie that I know he likes to work with –"

"I know which one you mean."

"Yeah, well, the two of them will show up on your doorstep and then everything you're worrying about will start to happen, real fast. They'll do both you and your little brother. I guarantee it – they like to do that sort of thing. So at least you won't have to worry about who's going to take care of him after you're dead. It won't be pleasant getting there, though, for either one of you."

"Okay –" I didn't want to think about stuff like that. "But –"

"Hold on." Cole held up a hand. "Just hear me out. Think about it. Somehow I manage to kill McIntyre for you, and maybe somehow along the way I can also drop our pal Michael and his little buddies off a roof – that's cool. I'd love to do that. Especially to that bastard Michael. He's the one who set me up. But everything that you and your brother would get, the whole bit of not having to worry about yourselves getting killed . . . I've already got that. I'm there right now." His hand swept toward the warehouse's empty spaces. "Long as I don't get all emotional and cranky, about having been made a cripple, and people I trusted screwing me over –" He shrugged. "I can go on like this for a long time. Like a permanent vacation. Got my girlfriend out there making some bucks, bringing 'em home, while I'm lying here all day drinking beer and catching up on the soaps – and some of those are pretty good, ya know – and I'm a happy camper. What's not to like?"

"Sure," I said. "If that's what works for you. If that's enough. I didn't think you were like that, though."

"Whether I am or not – let me tell you what doesn't work for me. What doesn't work is me doing whatever it takes to blow McIntyre away – and it doesn't happen. Because I'm not at the top of my game. Right?"

"Yeah, but . . . it's the kind of stuff you know how to do . . ."

"I also know how hard it's going to be. Given the shape I'm in. Let's just say you get me somewhere I can take a shot at him. And I miss. Then he's still alive. And way annoyed. Especially when he finds out that it was me who came after him. Think he's going to let me come back here and lie around, watching game shows and the Cartoon Channel? Believe me, I'd be screwed – and not in any of the fun ways."

I hadn't thought about any of that. Now I felt kind of self-centered.

"Matter of fact," said Cole, "I'd be doing myself a favor by taking Monica's cell phone and giving our old boss a call. I've still got his direct number. I'm sure he'd love to hear from me. Old times' sake, you know. Plus, I'm sure he'd get a kick out of how his former accountant dropped by my place and tried to hire me to kill him. Yeah, him and Michael would get a huge laugh out of that one. And McIntyre's the kind of guy who knows how to show his gratitude – you know, for bringing some sunshine into his life. He'd probably send over one of those big flat-screen TVs. I'd like to have one of those."

"Oh." The amount of stuff I hadn't thought about was starting to add up.

"Actually, I'd like to have one of those so much – it's the movies, that's what they're really good for – how do you know that I haven't already called McIntyre? And told him about these fun plans you're cooking up for him." Cole leaned toward me with his twisted smile. "How do you know I haven't done that, Kim?"

"I don't know," I said in a small voice.

"That's right, you don't. But you can relax. I'm still getting a kick out of this part of the whole process. I can always throw you under the bus later on." He lit up another cigarette. "Know why I'm telling you all this?"

"Probably because you want to make me feel like crap."

"Nah. I don't care that much –" A coughing spasm doubled him up for nearly a minute. "But here's the thing," he said as he straightened again. "You need to know that I'm actually putting a lot on the line here. I've got a lot to lose – and I'm not just talking about not getting a big-screen TV. I'm talking about what happens if things go wrong. I'm not worried about McIntyre wanting to kill you. That's your problem. I'm just not big on my getting killed."

"So what do you want to do?" My head felt as though it were filling like a backed-up sink drain. All kinds of tangled things were floating around in there, and I couldn't figure them out. "Just tell me."

"We'll get to that later."

"Crap." My shoulders slumped. Who knew that killing somebody was going to be this complicated?

"Let's talk about you," said Cole. "Just what exactly is it that you thought you could help me with? I mean, in terms of taking care of McIntyre."

"I don't know." I really didn't. "You're the professional at that sort of thing. You tell me."

"Work with me, Kim. You must have some idea about what it would take. That's why you came to see me, instead of – oh, I don't know; the Orkin bug man."

"Well . . ." Moving my thoughts around was like shoving giant blocks of granite around. "I guess . . . I could be your backup. Or something."

"Backup? What's that supposed to mean?"

"I'd . . . be there, I guess. When you're taking care of McIntyre. And . . . help you out. If anything went wrong."

"How would you do that?"

"Maybe . . . I'd have a gun."

"And you'd fire it at somebody?" He smiled. "Like Michael? Somebody like that?"

"If I had to."

"Don't make me laugh. You're all cold-blooded when it comes to hiring me to kill somebody for you. But actually coming down on someone yourself? That'll be the day."

I knew he was right. I was already starting to think I'd gotten in over my head, just having come this far.

"Besides – where would you even get a gun?"

I pointed around the space. "You've got plenty of them –"

"Not as many as I used to. Had to unload a bunch of equipment – even my ride. That really hurt. But that's what happens, you go to the hospital without insurance."

"Tell me about it. My brother's meds, they're just outrageous. And for most of them, there aren't any generics or –"

"Yeah, okay. That's not the main thing right now. What I was trying to tell you is that I don't have quite the armory I used to. Fortunately, I still know people who can use . . . certain items. And I got a good price for most of 'em. But if I were going to get you all strapped, I'd have to lay one of my favorites on you." He held up the black .357 he always kept nearby. "Something like this baby. If Michael or one of the guys spotted you holding a piece like this, it might slow 'em up enough for me to get off a shot. That might help. A little."

"Then what's the problem?" I reached toward the gun in his hand. "I'll take it."

"No, you won't." He pulled the gun away from me. "It's loaded. Ready to go."

"Unload it, then."

"No way. I'm not going in there with an empty piece – even if it's just you carrying it."

"Okay, don't unload it –"

"Yeah," said Cole, "and then I'd have to be watching my own back the whole time, wondering when you might accidentally fire it off."

"I'll be careful."

"Famous last words. For me, that is. Piece like this isn't a toy, sweetheart. And you'd find that out soon enough, if you were to fire it. You'd go flying backward and land on your butt a couple yards away. Seriously – giving you this gun would be like strapping a hamster to a skyrocket. Fun and all to watch, but I don't know if it'd help me get the job done. Not the one you're talking about."

"I could handle it." My voice sounded defensive even to my own ears. "I mean, if you showed me how."

"Show you how – right. And what else would you need from me?"

"I don't know. Whatever it would take . . . to get me ready."

"Get you ready? For what?"

"To help you," I said. "If you needed it."

"Oh, I see. You'd be my little assistant, huh? My backup. So tell me – do you want a two-week economy hit man course, or do you want the super deluxe-o professional assassin package?"

"Don't screw around with me."

Cole laughed. "Sweetie, I am not screwing around with you. But you are definitely screwing around with yourself. You don't want me to get you ready – whatever the hell that's supposed to mean. What you want is to be me. You want me to somehow turn you into me." He drew back and shook his head. "Can't be done."

"Why not?" It was a stupid question, but I had to ask it.

"Because you don't have what it takes. If I brought you along when I go after McIntyre – you'd just freeze up. You'd be no frickin' help at all to me. Because this isn't something that someone like you can do. That's why you became an accountant. If you had what it takes, you'd alreadybe me – or somebody like me. Even if you had a little bit of what it takes – there isn't time. McIntyre would be dead of old age before I could teach you everything you'd need to know."

"All right." I started to get up from the chair. "Sorry I wasted your time."

"Sit down."

I froze half-way up, then sat back down. "What? You're not done?"

"What I'm saying is that I can't turn you into me. But I can turn you into you. The real you. Maybe not a killer – but close enough."

"I don't think so." I felt tired already. "I don't think that's what I am. I don't even know what I am."

"The hell." Cole ground the cigarette butt out on the bare concrete at the side of the mattress. "Don't try to tell me my business. This is the stuff I know about. You remember what you told me, about when McIntyre fired you? When he told you about how you weren't getting the CFO job, that he was giving it to the Ivy League jerk instead?"

"Yeah. I guess so."

"You know what most women would've done, if that'd happened to them? They would've dissolved into a puddle. Boo hoo hoo. And McIntyre would've been handing them a tissue from the box on his desk. That's what most men would've done. Nobody puts up a fight anymore. Nobody. But what did you do?"

I didn't say anything. I was watching a movie inside my head, a short one, with just McIntyre and myself in it.

"You went for his throat," said Cole. "You launched yourself out of your chair – and went for the sonuvabitch. With your fingernails, like you were going to rip out his windpipe."

I looked straight at him. "You believed me about that?"

"Yeah. I did."

I wasn't sure if I believed it. Somebody had done it – gone for McIntyre's throat – but I wasn't sure if it had been me.

"The deal's off." I stood and started zipping up my jacket. "This was a bad idea."

"No, it's not." Cole held me transfixed with his slitted, unsmiling gaze. "It's a really good one. Because I can do it. If you help me."

I stood there listening to him.

"But it's going to take more than just me giving you a gun and showing you how to wave it around without hurting yourself – or me. We can do this thing, all right. But the only way we can do it is together. Got me?"

"I don't know what you're talking about."

"Dig it. You were right to come and talk to me. About what you want done. Maybe I can't walk anymore, but I can still shoot." He picked the .357 up again. "And you won't need to. It'll take some planning, but if you can get me someplace where I've got a shot at McIntyre, then he's a dead man. I don't care how many security people he's got around him."

"You said you were worried. About what would happen if you missed. And McIntyre was still alive."

"That was just talk," said Cole. "I just wanted to make sure you knew where I was coming from."

I finally understood that. And where he had been heading all along.

"Okay. Tell you what." I looked straight back at him. "You can shove this whole thing."

He smiled. "That doesn't sound like a little accountant girl talking."

"It isn't. It's me talking. Because here's what's going to happen."

Cole tilted his head to one side, one eyebrow lifting as though he were discerning something about me for the first time.

"We've got a deal," I said. "But I'm going to tell you what it is."

"Yeah?" He raised an eyebrow. "Hit me."

I stepped onto the mattress and looked down at him. "I'm not going to go through all this, then you're the only one who winds up getting to take a shot at McIntyre. So here's how we're going to do it. You won't be the only one taking a shot."

"What?"

"You heard me. I'll have a gun, you'll have shown me how to use it – and I'll be taking a shot at McIntyre, too."

"No, you won't. You don't have what it takes. And I can't give it to you."

"All right, then. I won't be able to. But it won't be because I don't know how to shoot some stupid gun."

"You know –" Cole looked up at me in disgust. "You're making things way more complicated than they need to be. This job's already going to be tough enough without some novice spraying bullets around me, while I'm trying to get some work done. No way."

"Then we don't have a deal." I turned and walked away, toward the door.

"Hold on." He called after me. "All right, all right. I'll show you how to use the piece – mainly to keep you from blowing my head off."

I didn't turn around to look at him. But I was smiling. Because all of a sudden I knew it didn't matter.

Maybe I wasn't a killer like him –

But I could dream about it.

SEVENTEEN

COLE GAVE me some homework. Something to take home and practice on.

"You need to start getting used to this." That was what he had said, when he had handed me the gun. There was a metal cabinet, on little rolling caster wheels, that he'd had me drag over to the mattress on the floor, so he could get into it. There hadn't been much in it – as he'd already told me, he'd had to sell off a lot of his equipment. But what there had been was another .357, not grimly black like his favorite that he always kept close at hand, but a gleaming brushed silver.

This is the problem with getting to some future utopia, with no guns and everybody just getting along with each other. The guns are just so much prettier.

I had stood there at the warehouse, weighing the .357 in my hands – it pretty much filled them up – while Cole had watched me.

"Just start getting your mind wrapped around it," he had told me. "Just the fact of it being around. We'll get to the actual firing-it-off part."

I had done as I was told, slipping the gun into my backpack. When I slung the pack's strap over my shoulder, I could feel the weight pulling me to one side, as though the earth's gravity had a new claim on me.

"What if I hurt myself with it?" He'd already raised that possibility.

"Try not to," Cole said dryly.

"No, seriously."

"Then we'll have learned something about you. That's progress, too."

Just strapping the backpack, with the gun inside it, onto the motorcycle's seat had been a new experience. I had worked my way out of the district by the wharves, then cruised carefully along the streets leading home, knowing the whole time that it was sitting back there behind me, like a coiled-hard snake.

"How'd it go?"

That was Donnie, hoping that my first day on my new job had gone well.

"It was fine," I said. "Just fine. Lot of stuff to get up to speed on, though."

"Wow." His nose wrinkled, and he actually scooted his wheelchair back a couple of feet. "You really smell like smoke."

I bent my head down and took a whiff from the front of my shirt. He was right.

"Yeah, well – that's what comes with working at places like that." I had told him before where I was going to look for a job. "The customers smoke, employees smoke – it's their world, and you're just in it."

I took a shower, to get the tobacco stink out. It was starting to make me nauseous as well. I could see that hanging around with Cole was definitely going to come with some negative side effects. I brought the backpack, complete with its heavy contents, with me into the tiny bathroom. I didn't want Donnie snooping around and finding the gun.

Two run-throughs with the shampoo were needed before I could stand myself. Toweling my hair dry, I regarded myself in the little mirror above the sink. I wasn't sure if the girl looking back at me was different or not. From what I'd been before. There was a way to find out, though.

The bathroom was so small that my backpack was right there on the tiled floor, next to my bare feet. I squatted down, unzipped the pack, and took out the big shining gun that Cole had given me.

Just holding it put my head in another strange space. I was pretty sure that having a boyfriend would've felt different – I wasn't that weirded out by the gun – but then again, how would I know? Not like I had much – or any – experience along those lines.

It wasn't the first time that I'd thought that girls like me have to take what we can get.

I stood up in front of the sink, dropped my towel, and inspected the result. The mirror was so small that the only way I could see myself and the gun at the same time was to bring it up close to my face. I was being careful – I set my finger on the trigger, but kept the gun pointed up at the bathroom ceiling. Just in case. I couldn't remember whether Cole had said anything about it being loaded or not, when he had given it to me.

With my other hand, I combed my hair down in front of my shoulder. That and the gun produced an interesting effect. Both inside and outside of me. Now I knew it was a different girl looking back from the mirror. This one wasn't a little nerdy accountant type, scared of her own shadow. This one was . . . different.

I looked down at myself. Even there. When you're as small as I've been my whole life, it's not like you're ever going to be packing around Dolly Parton-sized equipment. But there was something going on, that hadn't been before. I figured it must've been some hormonal response, though I wouldn't have expected it to kick in this soon.

Either that, or having the gun made me stand up straighter. Putting 'em out there, so to speak.

All this must've distracted me. Plus, giving something complicated as a gun to an inexperienced somebody like me – might as well hand a Lego set to a chimpanzee. Chances are good that pieces are going to go flying.

Which is what happened. Somehow, without trying to, my thumb poked a latch on the .357's gleaming flank, some major piece of it swung open, then there were bright, brassily gleaming bullets clattering on the bathroom tiles.

The bottom of my gut dropped a little, too. The thing actually had been loaded the whole time I was fooling around with it. What an idiot.

"Kimmie!" Donnie shouted from his bedroom. In a place this tiny, that was close enough for him to hear all the noise going on around me. Which included the thunk of me dropping the gun, as though it were a snake that had suddenly woken up in my hands. "What're you doing in there?"

"Nothing –" Down on my knees, I prodded the gun into my backpack, where I should've left it to begin with. "Don't worry about it." I scooped up the bullets and threw them in. If Cole was going to show me how to work this thing, he could start with the basics tomorrow. "Just . . . trying something new." I stood up and grabbed my bathrobe from the hook on the bathroom door. "That's all."

"Sounded like more than that." He gave me another one of those looks when I came out.

"New calculator." I snugged the robe's belt tighter around my waist. "For my new job. I was putting the batteries in, and I dropped them."

I don't know if I convinced him. But at least he didn't say anything more about it.

† † †

Next morning's session with Cole was shorter. Much shorter.

That was because we talked about money.

"We're going to need some," he told me. "A lot, actually."

"Wait a minute." When I had arrived at the warehouse, I had pulled the same chair from the wobbly table back over to the mattress. I was sitting on it backward, my arms laid across the top. "I said I was going to pay you – but there's a limit. You've got your reasons for wanting to kill McIntyre – and I've got my reasons for wanting to see that happen. That's got to be a big part of why we're doing all this."

"I wasn't talking about getting paid." Cole had set the overflowing ashtray on his stomach, as though it were a bowl of Cheerios. The rate at which he went through a pack of cigarettes these days, it probably made more sense than rolling to one side on the mattress to reach for the ashtray. "But there are expenses involved in an operation like this. Major expenses."

"Like what?"

"Excuse me – but is there some doubt in your mind about this? There shouldn't be. I'm the expert on the subject, remember? You came to me."

"I'm just asking." My hair swung forward, along the side of my face, as I shook my head. I hadn't pulled it into my usual skinned-back ponytail when I had gotten ready this morning. I had left it loose. "You don't have to jump down my throat."

"Fine," said Cole. "As long as we understand each other. You can consider this as part of your education."

"Lay it on me."

"Okay – we're talking about a hard target here. McIntyre, specifically. But the same rules apply, no matter who the target is. You think all that money you used to pay me, back when we were both working for McIntyre, you think that was all pure profit or something?"

I shrugged. "Never thought about it."

"You think about it now. Think about the expenses involved. There's the weaponry –"

"Don't we have that already?" I had set the clanking backpack down beside the chair.

"There're more things we're going to need besides the guns. There's all kinds of gear we'll have to have, if I'm going to get a fix on this guy – and get past his security systems, and his bodyguards, and everything else."

"You mean that bullethead Michael? That's who you're worried about?"

Cole leveled his hard gaze at me. "Tell you what," he said after a moment. "I guess I underestimated you. You seem to have already figured it all out. What do you need me for? Go ahead and take the gun I gave you, go on over there and blow McIntyre away yourself, then come back here and tell me how it went. I'd really like to hear it."

"All right, all right. I'm sorry. You're in charge."

That seemed to mollify him. At least for a while. To myself, I was starting to think that this was going to be a long course of instruction.

"So. Equipment." With a freshly lit cigarette, he gestured around the space. "How much of that do you see here?"

"I don't know." I obediently looked around, then back to him. "How much am I supposed to be seeing?"

"More than what's here. If I'd known you were going to be popping around here with this bright idea of you hiring me, then me going over and doing in our old boss – believe me, I wouldn't have sold off some of the pieces I did. Because some of that stuff would come in handy now."

I had no idea what he was talking about – at least in terms of specifics. What kind of equipment did he have before? Could've been remote-controlled Predator drones, for all I knew. I was just the one who'd written the checks that paid for it all.

"Okay," I said. "So we need to get stuff."

"Now we're making progress, sweetie. That's why I was talking money. We need it."

That, at least, there was nothing new about. Story of my life.

"How much are you talking about?"

Cole looked me straight in the eye. "How much you got?"

"Hm." I gave a slow nod. "I think you're the one who's getting a little off the mark now. You might be seriously overestimating the kind of savings account a girl would be able to scrape together, when she's been working for a tightwad like McIntyre."

"Not talking about your savings account. Not that I think you got one. I'm talking about the money you told me about, that you stole from him."

"I didn't steal it –"

"It's his money," said Cole. "And you've got it. Believe me, he's going to consider that as stolen. But you already know that. It's why you came to see me."

"Yeah, but –"

I shut up on my own. What I had been going to say was, But that's the money we're living on. I hadn't set it aside – or any of it – to be used for this new project of having him kill McIntyre.

I had to think about this. Which was hard to do while Cole was keeping his narrow-eyed gaze on me.

Say I spent all the money we had, the money in the envelope hidden in the bedroom closet, just handed it over to Cole to get the equipment he said he needed. And everything worked, and he killed McIntyre the way I wanted him to – then what? I supposed that if I didn't have McIntyre to worry about anymore, him and his crew, Michael and the other security types – then I could go out and get a regular job. Then maybe I could pay off what I'd then owe to Cole, for him killing McIntyre, on the installment plan. God only knew what the finance charges on something like that would be. It'd probably be like buying a car, with the interest mounting up to more than the principal.

Of course, even getting to that point was a big maybe – depending mainly on my being able to get a job, any kind of job, when all of this was over. And that would depend, I supposed, on how much potential employers knew about my recent past. Probably better to clam up about hiring someone to kill my old boss and just go back to being Little Nerd Accountant Girl. Well, maybe I wouldn't go back to the ponytail and the schlub outfits. But a colorful past that included getting people killed was probably best kept to myself. I was pretty convinced that wouldn't look good on the resume.

And what if they didn't work out? Our plans, that is. What if all the money in the envelope got spent for the equipment Cole said he needed – bazookas, nuclear submarines, whatever – and he didn't pull it off? And McIntyre was still alive? And, as Cole had hypothesized, seriously pissed? Maybe that hadn't been just talk coming from Cole; maybe he really was concerned about that. It would be just like McIntyre to get all cranked about a couple of ex-employees trying to kill him. Then the money would be gone, with Donnie and me in worse shape than before, unable to scrape up even Greyhound bus fare if we decided to make a run for it. All we'd be able to do would be to sit in our apartment and wait for Michael's knock on the door. Without even being able to go out to the corner store and pick up another carton of ice cream to tide us over.

These are the kind of meditations you get when your head's in a bad place. I finally wound up at the point where I figured that if Cole took his shot at McIntyre and he didn't pull it off, it'd be better if both of us got ourselves snuffed right there on the spot. Better than just waiting around for it, at least.

Either way, handing the envelope of money over to Cole, that amounted to serious doubling-down on this whole project, as some casino blackjack player might describe it. But there wouldn't be another hand dealt without doing that.

Which meant that I had to make a decision.

"All right," I said. Cole watched me as I got up from the chair. "I'll be back in a little bit."

† † †

I lucked out. Donnie was asleep when I got back to the apartment, even though it was the middle of the day.

Standing as quiet as I could in the darkened bedroom, I looked down at him on the bed. Sometimes things didn't go well during the night – sometimes the meds didn't work, sometimes other stuff – and then he didn't get any sleep and neither did I. At least he could make up for it during the day.

I went over to the closet and dug out the envelope from under the sweaters.

"Kimmie – what're you doing?"

His eyes were open when I turned around.

"Nothing." One of the sweaters had fallen to the floor. I retrieved it and used it to hide the envelope. I held the sweater up. "It got cold outside, so I had to come back for this. That's all."

He nodded drowsily, his eyelids already slipping down. He laid his head back on the pillow.

That was a long ride back to Cole's place. At every block, I could've turned the motorcycle around.

But I didn't.

† † †

"What's this?"

"What does it look like?" I still had my helmet in one hand. I hadn't strapped it to the seat the way I usually did. I'd dropped the backpack to the floor as soon as I had taken out the envelope. "It's money."

Cole should've been the accountant. It had taken him just a few seconds to riff through the bills and count them all up.

"No, it's not." His gaze locked on mine. "This is chump change."

A cold knot, increasingly familiar, formed again in my gut. "What do you mean?"

"God, sweetie, did you get screwed –" He shook his head wonderingly as he gazed at me. "This is what you managed to lift off McIntyre?" In one hand, Cole flapped the envelope and its contents back and forth. "What a joke. This is just about enough to piss him off – then again, if you'd swiped a nickel off him, that would've been enough. But it's not enough for me to kill him with." He tossed the envelope on top of the blanket covering his legs. "Not by a long shot."

I knew he was right. I felt sick. It had been a lot of money by the standards of the Little Nerd Accountant

Girl – the one who was still inside me – but not in the real world. I didn't know.

I just didn't know what killing someone cost. I'd never done it before.

"So what do we do now?"

Cole didn't answer. He just kept watching me.

"Guess we don't do anything." My voice had dwindled down to a whisper again. "I guess . . . I was just dreaming. That's all . . ."

He looked away for a moment, then back to me. His expression was different then.

Maybe he was afraid I'd start crying. When you've got your heart set on having somebody killed, it's a real disappointment when you find out it's not going to happen.

"Okay," he said at last. "Don't worry about it." He picked up the envelope, gave its contents another glance, then tucked it beside himself. "This'll get us started."

"But . . . what about the rest? That we need?"

"Let me think about it." He leaned back against the wall behind him and studied the smoke he exhaled up toward the ceiling. "There's always a way. Just . . . gotta find it . . ."

EIGHTEEN

WHEN I WENT over the next day, Cole told me the plan he'd come up with. To get more money.

"You gotta be kidding." I stared at him, appalled. "That won't work."

"Actually, it will." He brushed cigarette ash from the front of his T-shirt. "It wouldn't work for anybody else, but you've got a shot at it."

"This is crazy." The wooden chair creaked under me as I rocked back in it. "You're out of your mind."

"Maybe." He seemed to have heard that sort of comment before. "You have a better plan?"

That was the real problem. I didn't.

"All right," I said. "When do you want me to go do this?"

"Today would be good."

† † †

I hadn't ridden the motorcycle out of the city before. Out in the country – I could see why people like doing that. Zipping in and out of city traffic is cool enough, but you're always one driver on his cell phone away from death. I'd already taken one header on the pavement and wasn't looking forward to the next one. So getting out of town, to someplace where I could lean over the tank and roll on the throttle without worrying about landing under the wheels of some Escalade – that was nice.

If I hadn't been on my way to dig myself even farther into this mess, it would've been even nicer.

At least I hadn't had to go home and pull on my business-lady outfit. I had been able to leave straight from the warehouse, there by the wharves, wearing the jeans-and-jacket gear I already had on. The only change I made was to pull my hair back the way I used to wear it, when I had been Little Nerd Accountant Girl.

An hour or so later, I was slowing the bike down at the outskirts of a little town on the river. A little town now; there had been a time not long ago when it had been bigger. Now the factories were all shut down, every window broken out, the empty employee parking lots filled with weeds sprouting up through cracks in the asphalt, yellowed newspapers fraying against the sagging chain-link fences. The downtown area was all boarded-up storefronts, except for the Salvation Army thrift shop and the package liquor stores on opposite street corners.

There was one other place still in operation, right at the edge of what had been the business district. It looked the way it had before, when I'd had to come out here to balance some account ledgers for McIntyre. (His pet security thug Michael had driven me out in one of the company cars, which had made for a long, unpleasant ride, with some Canadian heavy metal CD on the stereo the whole way.) The faded, peeling letters on the inside of the one-story building's window read DELTA FREIGHT & STORAGE. Visible through the sagging blinds were a couple of desks and a row of old-school wooden filing cabinets with dead houseplants on top of them, a World War II-era rotating fan with rust-specked blades so big they could have come off a bomber plane, and not much else. Except dust. I remembered sneezing for days after my first visit there.

I parked the motorcycle in front, avoiding the broken Night Train bottles in the gutter, and pulled off my helmet. Just like before, everything was dead quiet all along the street.

Technically, the place wasn't really open for business. At least, not for anything legitimate. It was another one of McIntyre's fronts.

"Hello?"

A little bell on a spring coil had jangled when I'd pushed the door open. With just my head poked inside, I looked around.

"Mr. Pomeroy?"

I heard a toilet flush somewhere in back. A moment later, a pear-shaped old man, with straining suspenders and untied shoelaces, shuffled out, drying his hands on a paper towel.

"Whatever it is you're selling, we don't need it." He plopped himself down behind the least dust-covered of the desks. "So save your breath, young man."

"It's me, Mr. Pomeroy. It's Kim. Kim Oh. Remember, I came out before and –"

He'd dug out a pair of bifocals from the pinstriped jacket hanging behind him. He peered at me dubiously, then his jowly, baby-pink face brightened.

"Well, I'll be – you are!" He nodded happily. "Hey, it's good to see you. Been a while."

We'd hit it off, the one time I'd been out before. Half that time had been spent with him showing me photos of his grandchildren, the youngest of which he'd never actually seen in person, because his son and daughter-in-law lived all the way in Trenton, New Jersey, and never came to see him.

A couple of months later, my brother and I had gotten a Christmas card from him. Just signed by him, because his wife had died about six years before. Lonely people send out a lot of Christmas cards, or at least the old ones do. They've got the time.

"Yes, Mr. Pomeroy." I channeled what was left inside me of the Little Nerd Accountant Girl, giving him a big smile. "It has been."

"What brings you out here? Come on over and have a seat." He took a pile of old newspapers from the chair at the side of his desk. "Nobody said anything about you dropping by."

"Well . . ." I sat down with my hands in my lap. "There's a reason for that."

"So this isn't a business trip for you? Just social? Wonderful!"

"Actually, it is. Mr. McIntyre sent me here. There's . . . there's a problem."

"Really?" He frowned. "Like what?" The creases in his forehead deepened. "Wait a minute. You said McIntyre sent you?"

"That's right."

"Hm." Pomeroy slowly shook his head. "Because I heard . . . something different. About you."

I nodded. "I know what you heard. But I'm still working for Mr. McIntyre. Same as you."

"Gosh. That's . . . strange. That's really different. From what I got told."

"You were told what everybody else was told. There's a reason for that. It's what Mr. McIntyre wanted everybody to hear."

"I don't get it," said Pomeroy. "What are you talking about?"

"Everybody's supposed to think Mr. McIntyre fired me. That I'm not working for him any longer. But I am. This way, I can take care of what he wants me to look into. This little . . . problem that's come up."

"Yeah?" He looked over his half-rimmed glasses at me. "What kind of problem?"

"It's actually not little." I leaned closer to him. "You know the company's gone through a reorganization process."

"Oh, sure. Big changes."

"Well, some things came up when we started all that. We found out that there are some people stealing from him. Inside the company. People who work for Mr. McIntyre."

"Well, can't say I'm surprised. There was some funny stuff like that going on out here. Maybe ten years ago or so." He shook his head. "It got real bad. And we had to do the same thing – get 'em to trust somebody, who rolled over on them for us. Then they all sort of . . . disappeared. McIntyre did that."

"So you know what I'm talking about."

"Sure. These things happen. But McIntyre's lucky he's got somebody smart like you looking into it."

"I'm glad you understand." I reached over and laid my hand on top of his for a moment. "Mr. McIntyre told me you would."

"So exactly how are these people stealing from the company?"

"The usual." I gave another shrug. "Diverting funds, skimming off the top, pocketing, scamming – there are a lot of clever little squeezes like that. After a while, they add up to a lot."

"Been there," said Pomeroy. "You don't have to tell me. So if there's anything I can do to help McIntyre out – I mean, help both you and him – you just have to ask. And you've got it."

"That's wonderful. That means a lot to me." I let my smile go bigger. There was a visible effect on the old man, like turning a grow light on over a sickly plant, if any of the ones on top of the file cabinets had still been alive. "Because he's really counting on me to sort this out. And if I do . . ."

"Sure." All warm and paternal, he patted my hand. "You can count on McIntyre to show his gratitude. I've worked with him a long time – he's that kind of a guy." He leaned back in his chair. "So what exactly is it that I can do for you? Must be something we need to keep quiet on – otherwise you wouldn't have come down here to talk to me in person about it."

"Yes," I said, "that's absolutely right. We have to be very careful. So you can't tell anyone else about this."

"Okay." He nodded. "You got it. Shoot."

"I need your passwords and access codes. For all your accounts."

Pomeroy fell silent, mulling it over with a frown.

"I thought," he said, "you had all that stuff. So you could monitor it from the computer at your office. I mean . . . you're not there any more, of course, but couldn't the company have set you up with a computer link somewhere else?"

"I've got all that." I shook my head. "But that's just to follow the numbers. So I can see what you're doing out here, what's going in and out of the accounts. I've always had that. But I can't control the accounts. I can't move money in and out of them, route it from holding user to another. That's what I need."

"I don't get it." His frown persisted. "Why would you need to do that?"

"We're setting up a trap. For the people who've been stealing from the company. If I can route a piece of this branch's receipts from one account to another, I can red-flag whoever tracks that activity. These people are very clever, Mr. Pomeroy. They're smart enough not to try and steal from the company's main accounts. They scan for transactions at the fringes of the company's operations – like out here – and then they go after them. If you help us out with this, we'll be able to follow the trace back and see exactly who they are. And then –" I turned my voice serious. "Mr. McIntyre can take care of them."

"Yeah, I bet he will. Believe me, I know that about him, too. But I don't know . . ." Pomeroy shook his head again, still looking dubious. "Giving you those passwords – that kinda violates a lot of our security procedures. I wish somebody – I mean somebody else – had also gotten in touch with me about all this."

"They can't risk it. That's why I had to come out here on my own. If the people inside the company – the ones who're stealing from Mr. McIntyre – if they knew what we were setting up, then they'd know not to fall into the trap. We have to do it like this."

"Yeah, well . . . I suppose that makes sense." His expression brightened. "Hey, I know what. I'll give Michael a call. You know, McIntyre's head of security. He can vouch for you. Then we'll be good to go."

"No –" My mind went racing as I stopped Pomeroy's hand from reaching for the telephone on the desk. Cole and I hadn't thought of what I should do if this happened. "Michael . . ."

Pomeroy regarded me with a raised eyebrow. "What about him?"

"He's –" The answer struck me. "He's one of them. We think he's one of the bunch who've been stealing from the company."

"Whoa." That rocked the old man back in his chair. "Damn. That's serious."

"Yes. It is."

"He's a dangerous guy. Real hot-tempered." A glint of admiration showed in Pomeroy's gaze. "I can see why you want to keep this all quiet. If Michael were to find out what you're trying to do . . . trying to bust him and all . . ." Pomeroy gave a slow shake of his head. "You'd be in big trouble. Michael would come after you. Sure as anything."

"I know." Little Nerd Accountant Girl tried to be brave. "But I have to do it. For Mr. McIntyre's sake."

"Okay. I understand. I'll help you out." He pulled a legal pad from his top desk drawer and started scribbling on it with a leaky fountain pen. "This'll only be a minute . . . I got most of 'em in my head . . ."

A few minutes later, I was standing in the doorway, the folded piece of paper tucked inside my jacket.

"This your motorcycle?" Pomeroy pointed toward the Ninja at the curb.

I nodded.

"Okay . . ." His dubious voice sounded again. "You be careful on that thing, you hear?"

"I will," I answered obediently. "I always am."

"People get killed on 'em." He wrapped me in a bear hug, tight enough to almost break a rib. "And I don't want anything to happen to you." He put his hands on my shoulders and looked me in the eye. "You're important to me – you hear?"

Then I was on the bike. And on the road, heading back into the city. Doing the thing about trying not to think and just ride. I felt guilty about lying to him.

But when you're old and lonely . . .

It wasn't like he hadn't gotten anything out of the deal.

† † †

I went home first and verified everything.

Sitting at the table in the kitchenette, looking at the screen of the laptop I'd taken out of the bedroom – Donnie had given me some guff about needing to finalize his picks for his online NASCAR fantasy league – I punched in the numbers from the unfolded sheet of yellow legal-tablet paper. I held my breath . . .

And everything came up, just the way they should. Like a flower garden blooming. I still had so much of Little Nerd Accountant Girl in me, I suppose, that numbers could get me this excited. Just like in the movies, when the words Access Granted flashing on the screen meant that the secret agents and their hacker buddies could now get down to serious rock 'n' roll action.

I didn't move anything around, from one account to another – though I could've. I wasn't going to pull the trigger on that, though, until everything else that Cole and I had talked about was lined up. I logged out, switched off the laptop, and carried it back to the little table beside Donnie's bed.

"You're going out again?"

He saw me pulling my jacket on. "Yeah," I told him. "I got some errands to run. For my job."

"Kinda late." He pointed past me to the apartment's night-filled window. "You gotta go do it now?"

"Hey – I've told you how these places are. Clubs and stuff. They run pretty late hours."

I wasn't sure whether he was totally convinced or not. I locked the apartment front door from the outside, then headed downstairs with my helmet dangling from one hand.

† † †

Cole's girlfriend Monica was there, when I arrived at the warehouse. I saw her car parked at the curb. I didn't care. I was pretty sure there wasn't anything she didn't know about what we were doing.

"How'd it go?"

I started unzipping my jacket as I pulled the chair over from the table. In sweatpants and wifebeater undershirt, Monica was doing something with a skillet and some eggs, on top of the electric hot plate they kept over at the side of the space. She gave me a cool, unsmiling glance, but didn't say anything.

"Okay. I guess." I sat down near the foot of the mattress, laying my forearms across my knees. "I got the numbers, at least."

"That's cool." Cole nodded. "You checked 'em out?"

"Seem to be good." I shrugged. "For now."

"Yeah . . . that'd be the issue, wouldn't it?" Cole lit another cigarette from the butt of the previous one. "We're under a little bit of time pressure here. Especially now."

"What do you mean?"

"Just think about it," said Cole. "What're you planning on doing, to get me some money? Major money."

"Just what we talked about. Before I went out there. There are some pretty serious exchanges that go through the front Pomeroy's running. Big floats of cash. All I have to do is redirect his monthly transfer over to a dummy account where I can get it. That should be plenty for us."

"Sure. And then what happens when all that money doesn't show up in the company account? Then what happens?"

This was something we hadn't talked about, but I wasn't worried about it.

"Nothing," I said. "At least not for a while. That account doesn't get reviewed 'til next quarter. The audit will take six months at the least. Believe me, I know; I set up the procedure. So we've got plenty of time."

"No, we don't."

"Who's the worry-wart now?" I couldn't believe this from him. "What're you getting into such a sweat over?"

"Simple," said Cole. "McIntyre might not know yet that you ripped him off, but your pal Pomeroy at the front does. I can guarantee that right now he's thinking about this whole deal. Now that you're not there to charm him with you sweet little schoolgirl routine. And he's getting nervous about it."

"Yeah, but –"

"But nothing. Sooner or later he's gonna check it out, one way or another – even if he has to go right up to McIntyre himself and tell him what the two of you did. That's way better than sitting around sweating and waiting for McIntyre to find out on his own. And as soon as he does that, then McIntyre knows, doesn't he?"

"Crap." I could barely see in front of myself. And I was sweating. I knew, with sudden and complete conviction, that Cole was right. "Why'd you talk me into doing this? You should've told me –"

"If I had, you wouldn't have gone out there and done what you needed to do. You woulda froze. And that wouldn't have gotten anything done for us."

"I thought we were partners." My seething glare could've killed him, if anybody's could. "And you didn't say anything about this."

"Relax." Cole smiled. "I said that we under pressure, not that we're totally screwed. That's how these things work in this business. You get yourself into a tight spot, then you get yourself out of it. There's no other way to get what you want. What we need."

"I'm not in the mood for a philosophy lecture right now."

"Good – because this is all practical, not theoretical. Here's the deal. We got a little time before the whistle gets blown. I know old guys like that, how their minds work. Matter of fact, I know your pal Pomeroy. I did some work out there, a while back. Did he ever mention to you something about a couple of guys ripping the company off, from before?"

"Yeah. He did."

"I'm the one who cleaned all that up. If those smart guys aren't around anymore, it's because I put the hammer on 'em. No big deal, it's what I do – or I used to – but I can tell you, the whole time I was out there, Pomeroy was sweating buckets. What can I say?" Cole shrugged. "Old guys get nervous. The smaller the amount of time that people figure they've got left to live, the more they worry about it. Problem with getting nervous, though, is that's when your mind shuts down. At least for a while. You gotta move, but you can't get off the dime."

That much, I knew about. From inside.

"So for the next coupla days," continued Cole, "your pal's gonna be sweating and thinking, but not doing anything. Even if he's totally convinced himself that you ran a number on him to get those account passwords. Better to call up McIntyre and fess up about what's he's done, or just sit there and hope that he's wrong about you and that it'll all blow over? That's what he's going to be dithering about. That's what gives us our chance."

"Chance to do what?"

"Concentrate, Kim. The money – that's what we're doing. Tomorrow morning, you make the transfer, then you go downtown to the bank where the dummy account is registered, and you draw the cash out. A nice fat wad of cash. You come on back here with it. Then we're done with that part of the whole process. And we're ready to roll on to the next part. Which – I promise you – will be more fun. That's the point where I start getting ready to kill our old boss."

Every working girl's dream come true. That thought cheered me up a little bit.

It didn't last.

"Wait a minute," I said. "What if you're wrong?"

Monica dragged over the other chair from the wobbly table, while balancing two plates of scrambled eggs on her arm, waitress-style. She sat down and handed one of the plates to Cole.

"Your partner here worries an awful lot." Monica pointed at me with her fork, then took another bite of the eggs. "Is she like this all the time?"

"Pretty much." Cole sprinkled Tabasco on his plate, from the little bottle that Monica had tossed to him. "But we're working on it." Mouth full, he looked across at me. "What if I'm wrong about what?"

"About Pomeroy being nervous. I mean, about how long it takes him to get over his nerves and give McIntyre a call?"

"Then I'm wrong about it. Big deal." Cole alternated between bites and drags from the cigarette he kept balanced on the edge of his ashtray. "Then McIntyre's watching the accounts, and he sees what you're doing with them. So when you go downtown tomorrow morning to draw out the money, Michael and one of his security crew are waiting there for you. They grab you and take you away."

"Then what?"

"What do you expect? Then you're dead."

My incredulous gaze traveled between the two of them, calmly finishing off the scrambled eggs. "You seem awfully okay with that."

"Actually, I'm not." He set the empty plate down beside the mattress. "Believe me, if that's what happens, I'll be just as disappointed about it as you. I mean, as you would be if you were still alive. You're the best shot I've got right now, for helping me to off McIntyre."

"Great." I couldn't keep the disgust out of my voice. "I'll try not to mess it up. For your sake."

"You do that."

Monica got up and carried the plates to the sink in the bathroom.

"Go home and get some sleep." Cole switched on the little portable TV and turned his attention to it. The yammering sound of Dancing with the Stars filled the space. "You've got a big day tomorrow."

I grabbed my helmet and stalked out.

NINETEEN

I WAS getting on the motorcycle when a hand grabbed my elbow.

This late at night, I hadn't brought down the visor of my helmet. By the yellow glow from the one functioning streetlight at the end of the block, I could see it was Monica.

"Didn't you hear what he said?" I nodded toward the warehouse door. "I have to get home and get my beauty sleep. Want to look my best, if I'm going to get my head blown off."

"Look," she said. "You don't have to tell me what a jerk the guy is. I've been hooked up with him for years. Believe me, I would know."

"Then you've had time to get used to him." I kept my grip on the handlebars. "Or at least resigned. I haven't."

"You will. Unless you're careful."

"What's that supposed to mean?"

"We need to talk." Monica held up a couple of beers that she'd taken from the little camping fridge plugged inside the warehouse. "Come on."

"No thanks," I said. "I'm still underage."

"Yeah, right. You're putting together your plans to kill somebody, then you're worried about being a minor caught with a brewski in her hand. Get real. Anybody sees us, I'll tell 'em I'm your mom."

"Then you'd get charged with endangering the morals of a minor."

"Honey, your morals have already crashed. And you're just climbing out of the wreckage of them."

"Whatever." I gave up. I pulled the helmet off my head and set it on the motorcycle seat behind me. I nodded as I looked at her. "Yeah, the family resemblance is obvious."

Monica twisted off the cap of one of the beers and held it out to me. I got off the bike and took the beer from her.

"Let's go for a walk," she said. "Helps you think."

Little Nerd Accountant Girl had had a beer, or anything alcoholic, maybe once or twice before in her wildly adventurous life. I hadn't cared for it then, but this night it seemed to hit the spot. One that I hadn't known existed before. If nothing else, it sluiced the taste of cigarette smoke off the tongue, that you pick up just from hanging around somebody who's smoking up a forest fire. Now I could see why the stuff's popular in bars.

We walked along the empty industrial district streets, past the locked-up freight haulers and the clusters of identical white panel vans behind more chain-link fences. Monica kept silent, just taking a swig from her own green bottle now and then. She seemed to know where she wanted to get to.

Which turned out to be the pilings at the foot of the nearest wharf. We sat down there and watched the slow, listless waves deposit more oil-slicked rubbish on the wet gravel below us. Out on the water, the big black silhouettes of container ships blocked out the city lights.

"All right," said Monica at last. Holding her beer by the neck, she swirled the last inch around inside. "Here's the deal. You know why I'm still hanging out with Cole? I mean, given his condition, he's not exactly a prime catch. Is he?"

"I don't know." I had been leaning forward, forearms on my knees, dangling my own bottle before me. I glanced over at Monica. "Maybe . . . you're loyal or something. Something like that."

I didn't even know why she was asking the question. If I'd ever known why anybody did anything, I probably wouldn't have been in the situation I was in now. You might as well ask your house cat how to do algebra. You'd have a better shot at getting an answer.

"Sure," said Monica. "Like I can afford stuff like that. Nobody can. That's why you don't see it very often."

Right now, I was just hoping that I wasn't going to wind up sitting here, listening to her problems. I had enough of my own.

"Okay," I said. "So why then?"

"Simple." She took another swig. "I don't have any options. When you don't have options, you do what's left. I hooked up with Cole, then things happened – things you don't need to know about – and then one day there weren't any other options. There was just him."

"That kind of sucks."

"No . . ." She shook her head. "It's not so bad. We've had some fun. But it's the kind of fun you have when you don't have any other choice."

"Well . . ." I tried to think of something to cheer her up. "I haven't even had that kind of fun."

"You've got something else. You've got options."

"I do?" I hadn't thought about it.

"Even now. Even this far along in the process." She pointed with her thumb down the way we had come. "You could go back there right now and get on that little motorcycle of yours, go home, and get your little brother and strap him on to it, then just head out. Just get on the highway and go, for as long and as far as you can.

People do that kind of thing all the time. That's what I did when I was your age."

"Okay." I gave a slow nod. "Not to be rude or anything – I mean, I appreciate your advice and all – but isn't your having done that kind of how you wound up with somebody like Cole?"

"Good point." She took another drink. "You're thinking. That's good. That was never much of a habit with me."

"I don't know – it's not like it's done me that much good so far."

"That's because you haven't thought enough. About what's going to happen. If you go along with all this stuff that you and Cole have cooked up. Correction, honey – that he's cooked up. You don't know half of what he's thinking and planning."

I didn't bother pointing out that I pretty much didn't know anything about what Cole was planning. Other than going to the bank tomorrow morning and either walking out with a bundle of money or getting myself killed. After that, the agenda was pretty opaque.

"You don't even know," said Monica, "what he's planning for you."

"Guess I'll find out." If I were still alive for that part.

"You don't have to. Like I said, you've got options. All this stuff that you've told yourself, and that Cole has told you, that you don't have any other choice except to have him go after McIntyre – that's all crap. The only reason you're telling yourself all this stuff is because it's what you want to do."

"Okay." I shrugged again. "Then it's what I want to do. What's the problem with that?"

"The problem is that it means your head's kinda messed up."

Not telling me anything new there.

"There's no future in this stuff," said Monica. "Look at what happened to Cole."

"Give me a break." I lowered the bottle after taking another swig. "I just want to have somebody killed. Just one. It's not like I'm planning on making a habit out of it."

"That's what you think." Her voice turned dark-shaded. "Cole started out with options, too."

"I'll try to bear that in mind."

"Maybe he's right about you." She gave me a hard look. "Maybe you're just about as cold-hearted as he thinks you are. With all this having someone killed stuff and all."

"Yeah, well, maybe it's just a phase I'm going through."

I was getting close to the end of the bottle. When you're as small as I am, one's enough. Or a lot.

"He sees something in you," said Monica. "That's probably not good."

"What kind of something?"

"What the hell do you think?" She gave a quick laugh. "Something like him. Like what he's got. Though frankly . . ." She studied me for a moment. "I can't see it. Messing with people's not what I would've thought you'd be good at. Maybe he thinks you've got some sort of built-in kung fu ability or something."

"That's Chinese." I shook my head in amazement. "What is it with you people? If there were an exhibit at the natural history museum marked Dumb Round-Eyes, you and your boyfriend would be in it."

"Huh. Oh isn't a Chinese name?"

"Not in my case. It was Oh-Seon or Oh-Seong or something like that, when my grandparents came over from Korea."

"Fine, great. Have it your way. But still – isn't there some sort of crazy Korean martial art?"

"Yeah, we call up our cousins in Pyongyang and have 'em launch a nuclear strike on Tokyo. How the hell would I know?"

Monica's laugh was beer-tinged as well. "You're kind of a bust at being Korean. If that's what you are."

"That's because I'm not. I'm not even Korean-American."

"What are you then?"

"I don't know." It hadn't taken much alcohol to unlock a little door inside me, that I would just as soon have kept closed. Even if I had known it was there. "I'm just like everybody else – I'm not anything. Maybe we're all just Feral-American now. You know what feral is?"

She nodded. "Wild dogs."

"Cats, too. Any kind of animal. Just abandoned, left out on their own. That's what we're all like. No wonder everybody's so screwed up. Nobody tells us what we should do, what we should even freakin' be. Like if there was supposed to be some bundle of ancestral Korean wisdom, I sure as hell didn't get one. I gotta try and figure out everything on my own, just like everybody else has to. You know what that's like?"

"Sure –"

"I'll tell you what it's like." Something unrestrained came bursting out of that unlocked door inside me. "When I was a kid, I mean a little kid, like fourteen or something – a couple of the foster parents who were taking care of me and my brother, they dragged us to some Methodist church every Sunday. And I wound up in the choir. Not because I could sing, but because having me in the front row made it look all diverse and stuff. Like Token Asian Kid. They liked that sort of thing. And then –" I drained the last of the beer and slung the bottle into the water. "The freakin' choir goes to Spain. To sing at some dopey festival. I don't even remember it. But I'll tell you what I do remember. What I remember is that we all took some train ride, when we weren't singing, to go look at some cathedral or something. And we wound up at some train station in some little town in the middle of nowhere. I had to take a pee, and I knew just enough tourist Spanish to know which was the ladies room. I go in there by myself – and there's a freakin' hole in the floor! That's the plumbing. And I'm standing there, this fourteen-year-old girl, a million miles from home – a million miles from Korea, for that matter – and I'm looking at this hole in the floor. And believe me, it's not a pleasant hole – it looks like people have been doing something in it since Year One. Only I don't know what it is. What I'm supposed to do with it."

The empty beer bottle had landed with a splash. The oily water, glistening in the moonlight, smoothed out again.

"And that's what it's like," I said. "My whole life. That's what it's like for everybody, I guess. All the time. It's like being a fourteen-year-old girl who has to pee, and you're someplace where you don't even know how that's done there, and you have to figure out on your own how to pee!" I shook my head. "I don't think that's right."

"But it's the way it is."

"Yeah." I took the bottle out of her hand, tilted my head back to drain the last bit, then threw the bottle after the other one. "It's the way it is."

"So that's why you're listening to Cole. And hiring him to kill somebody."

"I guess so." I hadn't really thought about it before. "I mean . . . yeah, he's kind of a psychotic and stuff. And he kills people – or he used to. So at least something is happening."

"And that's good enough for you."

"I don't know." Whatever had been inside me was gone, leaving me unfortunately sober again. "I suppose I'll find out."

"Sure." Monica stood up from the piling on which she had been sitting. "You want to know something else?"

"No. But go ahead and tell me, anyway."

"You didn't say anything I didn't already know you were going to say. About you and Cole . . . and all of it. Except for the peeing thing. That was a little strange. But all the rest of it . . . I already knew that was where you're at. I just didn't want you to be able to say that nobody ever warned you."

I slowly nodded, looking out at the water.

"Come on." Monica started walking back toward the warehouse. "Big day tomorrow."

TWENTY

WEIRD THING was that it wasn't a big deal at all.

The bit at the bank – it went off with no problem.

Maybe that's a tribute to good grooming. I had put on the business-lady outfit in the morning. And I had left the Ninja parked a few blocks away from the bank, so nobody would see me getting off of it.

Probably also a tribute to being a little Asian chick. You can fly under people's radar that way. When you're my size, nobody expects anything bad from you. Which is an advantage.

Of course, the whole time I was sweating. Especially when the bank staff took me to a private office. You withdraw that much money from an account, they don't stack it up for you at one of the teller cages.

"Are you sure you wouldn't rather have a cashier's check?"

Sitting in front of the bank official's desk, I was afraid that at any moment Michael and his fellow security thugs were going to burst out of the oak-paneled walls. These people might have been just messing around with me, lulling me into thinking that everything was going along fine, just so they would enjoy it more when the hammer came down on me.

"No, I'm afraid it'll have to be cash." I was mainly concentrating on keeping my cool, refraining from running out of the bank in a sudden panic. "My client is rather . . . eccentric." To say the least.

"It'll take a few minutes. I hope you don't mind waiting."

"Not at all." I handed over the empty briefcase I had just bought at the office supplies store along the way. "I understand."

What else I learned that morning? You overdraw your checking account by five bucks, you get treated like dirt. Because you're nobody. Ask for a wad bigger than the annual budget of some Third World nations, and you're somebody. You get treated different.

A quarter of an hour later, and I was out of there. The sun shone on me as I walked along the downtown sidewalk. Michael and his thugs were nowhere in sight.

My spirits lifted. Maybe, I thought, just maybe – it's all going to happen. Carefully, I strapped the locked briefcase to the motorcycle seat, pulled on my helmet, and headed for the wharves.The way it's supposed to.

I was about to find out otherwise.

† † †

"Nice job." Cole sat on the mattress, with the briefcase on his lap. "I knew you wouldn't have any trouble."

"You knew?" I stood looking down at him. "Then what was all that last night? What were you getting me all cranked up for?"

"Think of it as practice." He closed the lid on the money. "Practice being tense. It'll come in handy later. Not everything's going to be a piece of cake like this."

About then, I was wondering how much I'd screw up my karma if I kicked a cripple's ass.

"Fine," I said. "Enjoy that. I've had enough for today. I'm going to go home."

"No, you're not. No time for kicking back. We've got some work to take care of – or at least you do."

"Now what?" Even if everything had gone all right, the whole business at the bank had worn me out. All I wanted to do was go home, pull off this stupid panty hose, make lunch for Donnie and me, then fall asleep on the couch. "Can't it wait?"

Monica stepped out of the bathroom. She obviously had just finished putting on her exotic dancer makeup, getting ready for work.

"I'll leave you people to it." She took her jacket from the hook it was hanging on. "Have a good time. Try to leave a couple of walls standing, at least."

I looked back at Cole when she had left. "What was that supposed to mean?"

"It means the job you're going to work on now." Cole laid the briefcase at the side of the mattress. "Where's the gun?"

"What gun?"

"The .357. The one I gave you."

I had actually left it in my backpack, strapped to the seat of the motorcycle, when I had gone into the bank. That'd seemed smarter than carrying it with me. I don't care how well-dressed you are, withdrawing large sums of money while packing is probably not a good idea. Unless you've got your panty hose pulled over your head.

"Right here." I slung my backpack from my shoulder. "I don't think I broke it."

"Broke it?" Cole leaned forward to take the pack from my outstretched hand. The gun clanked heavily against the bullets rattling at the bottom. He unzipped the backpack and looked inside. "Goddamn it, Kim. It's not a toy."

"Well, screw you, too." I was not only tired, I was getting irritated. "It's not like you gave me the instruction manual with it."

"The instruction manual begins now. Come over here."

"And do what?"

He sighed and shook his head. "Just sit down. And watch and learn."

I sat down on the floor beside him. There didn't seem to be any way around it.

"All right." Cole spread the gun and its pieces on the blanket, along with the bullets. "Here's how you get a piece ready for business . . ."

† † †

That took hours.

By the time we were done, I might not have been able to take the .357 apart and put it back together in the dark – and I wouldn't have won any speed trials while doing it with the lights on – but at least I wasn't a complete embarrassment anymore.

"So are we done?"

Cole shook his head. "We haven't even started. Now we get to the fun part." He picked the shiny weapon up from the blanket and handed it to me. "Stand up."

I let the gun dangle at my side. "Now what?"

"Imagine McIntyre's standing over there." From the mattress where Cole was sitting, he pointed to the far wall of the warehouse. "See him? Now let 'er rip."

"What?" I looked from him to the wall and back again. "You mean shoot?"

"No, I mean run over there, and hit him in the head with it. Yeah, shoot."

"Why?"

"Because –" Cole spoke with elaborate, condescending patience. "When you shoot somebody, that's how you kill them. If you do it right."

"Yeah, but . . . I'm not going to be the one who does that. You are."

"Maybe so. But to get me to where I can do that, you're gonna have to be there. And yeah, I appreciate all the confidence you have in me and all, but like I told you before – things could go wrong. And then I'll need you to help me out. The only way you can do that is if you're also carrying a piece. Even if you don't fire it off – and believe me, I really hope you don't. For mysake. So the only way to avoid some major screwup is for you to at least know how to handle the thing."

I looked down at the gun in my hand. It seemed really big, heavy and intimidating. At least to me, it did.

"I can't hit anything from here." I looked up at him. "I've never –"

"Even you can hit a wall. I promise you. If not, we're going to have to seriously rethink our plans."

I turned and slowly raised the gun.

"Hold it with both hands," instructed Cole. "Don't lock your arms like that. Or you really will land on your butt."

This was a new thing. But in some ways, it wasn't. Because I'd been dreaming about something like this. And here it was at last.

"Like I showed you. Just squeeze . . ."

"Wait a minute." I lowered the gun and looked back at him. "Isn't somebody going to hear this?"

"Sweetie, in this neighborhood you could fire off a howitzer and nobody would care, long as you weren't pointing it at them. Quit fooling around and shoot."

I brought the gun up again in both hands, braced myself with one foot behind me, and squeezed the trigger –

"Crap!" The shot was still echoing inside the warehouse. "What the hell . . ." The gun itself had come within inches of clopping me on the forehead. My arms ached all the way back to my shoulder blades. "That sucks."

"You'd better get used to it," said Cole. "What did you think it was going to be like?"

"Dunno." There was an impressive hole punched into the wall. "This is the same kind of gun you use?"

"Yeah – I never had any problem with it."

"Well, sure. But you're a guy. You got some weight going for you. Plus all that upper body strength. I think I need a girl's gun."

"I think you need to suck it up and stop whining. You'll get used to it."

"I don't think so . . ."

"Don't worry," said Cole. "There's a trick to it. Once you figure that out, then there's no problem."

"Yeah?" I looked up from the gun in my hand. "What's the trick?"

As usual, he couldn't just tell me what I wanted to know. "When you were in school, did you do any sports?"

"Only in P.E. Like volleyball and stuff."

"Any good at it?"

"No," I said. "I sucked. There were always these corn-fed amazons who'd spike the ball into my face. After the first couple of bloody noses, I'd just dive for the floor."

"See? You didn't learn the trick back then."

"Which is?"

"You gotta hate the other guy more than you love yourself."

That actually made sense. It sounded like something I could do. "And that'll help me with the gun?"

"No, but it'll help you get in the practice you need." Cole pointed to the wall. "Fire off another one."

The second time wasn't any less jarring than the first. My ears were ringing.

"Uh . . . just how good am I going to have to be at this?" I had lowered the gun. "I mean, yeah, I've hit a wall twice in a row, but I don't think I'm ready to knock a fly out of the air."

"Not an issue." Cole dug out his lighter. "Like you said – when we go to see McIntyre, you're not going to be the one doing the dirty work. Right? Just backup. So don't worry about being an expert like me." He pointed to the wall with the lit cigarette. "Fire off the rest, then we'll reload. And you can do it again."

"You're kidding." I stared at him. "This is the biggest waste of time –"

"Yeah, but –" I couldn't keep my voice from slipping into its whining mode. "My arm hurts. And my ears are ringing . . ."

"Either you hate him enough – or you don't."

"All right." I turned around and raised the gun again in both hands . . .

† † †

By the time Cole let me quit, the floor was littered with empty ammo cartons.

Plus, I'd had to go through his whole elaborate gun-cleaning ritual twice. If I'd known how much housekeeping was going to be involved, I might not have put in for this gig.

"So we're done?" Sitting cross-legged at the end of the mattress, I dug the wads of balled-up toilet tissue out of my ears. I could see through the warehouse's dust-clouded skylights that it had gone dark outside. "I can go home now?"

"Oh, you can go, all right." Cole had filled up his ashtray again. "But not home."

I laid down flat on my back, my hands outstretched, the weight of the .357 filling one. "Now what?"

"You have to go back out there. And plug that hole."

"Hole?" My eyes went wide as I stared up at the warehouse ceiling. Something in his voice creeped me out. "What hole?"

"Pomeroy."

"What're you talking about?" I sat up, wrapping my arms around my knees. "We're done with him. I took care of all that." I pointed to the briefcase sitting against the wall. "So we could get the money."

"That was temporary," said Cole. "I'm talking about permanent."

"I don't get it. What exactly is it that needs to be taken care of? He's just an old guy, sitting out there."

"Correction. That's what Pomeroy used to be. Now he's an old guy sitting out there, who just let some young cupcake talk him into handing over his transfer account passwords. The ones that his boss McIntyre uses to move his money around. A whole bunch of which is no longer sitting in the bank where it's supposed to be. It's in that briefcase over there."

"Yeah, but . . . but that was the plan . . ."

"No. That was part of the plan. Now we have to move on to another part of the plan. Or rather – you do."

"Wait a minute. He trusted me."

"Gosh. Guess that was a mistake."

"But . . ." My mind was racing again. "I thought we were just going to let him be. Because he'd be scared to go tell McIntyre what he'd done. And that'd keep him quiet."

"Sure, that might keep him quiet. It might even have kept him quiet long enough for us to do what we want to McIntyre. If you hadn't gone down there and taken that money out of the bank. But Pomeroy still has those passwords, too. He still has access to those accounts. When he sees how much got disappeared from them, yeah, he'll still be scared. He'll be scared spitless that McIntyre is going to think he took that money."

Inside my head, I could see the gears lining up and meshing.

"And that's a death sentence, sweetie. For him." Cole took a long drag from his cigarette. "He's not going to sit out there and wait for Michael and his crew to show up. He's going to roll over on you. That's the only way he can save himself."

I couldn't say anything. I couldn't even see anything.

"For all we know," said Cole, "your friend Pomeroy might have checked those accounts today. While we were doing our indoor gun range practice. And he's calling up McIntyre right now."

"You sonuvabitch." I managed to bring him into focus. "You set me up. You knew this would happen."

"I didn't set you up. You did. If you couldn't see this coming . . ." He sat back against the wall, flicking ash from his cigarette. "You got a lot to learn."

"This is crazy. I can't . . . I can't do that."

"Better you should learn now. When it's just an old man who has to be taken care of. Then you might be ready for the tough job."

I nodded slowly. Not thinking . . . just listening. To my own pulse.

"So . . ." I managed to say something. "What exactly . . . do I have to do . . ."

Cole reached over and took the .357 out of my hand. He flipped it open, found a fresh box of ammo, and started loading it up.

TWENTY-ONE

I JUST rode.

And thought.

After the accident, I had decided it was better not to do that. Better to just ride and keep my mind blank, no emotions, no words, no thoughts, no pictures. But I couldn't do that this time. There was too much going on inside my head.

The motorcycle's headlight gathered up the road ahead of me. Heading out of the city, the unlit highway cutting toward the river and the derelict small town. I'd know I had gotten there when I could see the big hulking shapes of the abandoned factories, the moonlight glittering on their broken windows.

There was someone else's voice that I could hear, as I leaned over the tank, shielding my face behind the windshield. Not Cole's voice, telling me what I had to do. It was Monica's.

When you don't have options . . . you do what's left.

I knew that was true. I knew it because in this world, the one I had worked so hard to get myself into, things like that are true.

But Monica had also told me something else. That it was different for me.

Even now. Even this far along . . .

I rolled the throttle on even more as I brought the Ninja out of a swooping curve. Just a few days ago, going this fast, speeding through the night – that might've scared me. But not now.

The world scared me.

This world – Cole's world – was a bad place. I'd succeeded in getting into it, becoming part of his world. And now . . .

Now I wanted out.

That was what I had decided. That was what my own voice, when I could hear it, spoke inside my head.

I wasn't a killer. That was a joke. I knew that now. It was a joke that I'd gone along with, because it was exciting. Everybody thinks about having their boss killed. Maybe, in their wildest fantasies, even doing it themselves. Imagining what it'd be like, to kill somebody who had screwed them over the way I had been screwed. But then all of a sudden, it was going to happen! Brave Little Nerd Accountant Girl – she wasn't going to be the one to actually pull the trigger, but she'd be there when it all went down. I'd even get to wave a real gun around, just like I knew how to use it . . .

Well, maybe I did. I did now. But I wasn't going to.

† † †

I spotted faint light leaking between the blinds. It slipped through the letters spelling DELTA FREIGHT & STORAGE, forming thin strips on the sidewalk in front of the building.

At the curb, I leaned the Ninja onto its kickstand and pulled off my helmet. I sat it on top of the backpack strapped to the seat and walked over to the door.

I'd figured I had a good chance of catching Pomeroy, still there at his shabby office. I knew he worked late – he didn't like returning to an empty house, so he put it off as long as possible. He'd told me that.

The door was unlocked. I pushed it open and looked inside.

"Mr. Pomeroy?"

The overhead fluorescent panel was switched off, so the only light came from the single green-shaded lamp on the desk. The old man sat there in the dim circle, making check marks on some papers.

He looked up at me. "Hello, Kim."

I knew then. Because he wasn't surprised to see me. Wasn't surprised that I had come all that way to talk to him. It meant that he knew. Everything.

"I'm sorry, Mr. Pomeroy." It was all I could think of to say. "I'm really sorry."

"That's all right. Things happen. People make bad decisions . . . all the time." A sad little smile appeared on his face. "I just wish . . . that when things had gone wrong for you . . . that you'd come out sooner and talked to me. Maybe I could've helped." He shook his head. "You didn't have to do all this other stuff."

"I know." My voice was quiet and small. "I know that now."

"It's a real mess," he said. "You shouldn't have done it. But I'll talk to McIntyre. He and I are old friends. We go back a long ways. I'll talk to him . . . and things will get sorted out. Don't worry about it."

That was what I was hoping to hear. I was going to get a break. The kind that killers don't get. The kind that foolish little girls, who get in way over their heads, sometimes get. If they're lucky, and if people – the ones who really own this world, like McIntyre – are kind to them. That was the most I could hope for. If I could just get that tiny bit, then maybe my brother and I would be okay. We could huddle down in our little corner of the world, just the two of us. And if we didn't bother anyone, anyone who really mattered, then maybe we'd be all right. Even if just for a little while.

"Are you sure?"

"Yeah, Kim, I'm sure." He pushed his chair back and got to his feet. "Come here. It's okay."

I stepped toward him as he smiled and spread his arms wide for a hug.

When the flat of his hand struck me across the face, I wasn't ready for it.

Pomeroy might've been an old man, but he was still strong. Strong enough to send me flying. I hit the floor and skidded, one shoulder and the back of my head bumping against a file cabinet.

"You stupid little . . .!" He towered over me, his panting breath straining the suspenders over his gut. "Could've gotten me killed!"

His shouting voice seemed to come from miles distant. The room tilted around me, and I could taste the wet salt of blood in my mouth.

"Think you were so smart!" His shoe drew back, then kicked me in the ribs. I gasped as I rolled onto my side, blindly scrabbling at the floor to get away from him. The next kick hit me in the back, sending a white bolt up my spine. "Think you could come out here and make a fool outta me – oh yeah, you think you're so cute. Think all you have to do is look at me and smile. That'll do it for an old bastard like me, huh?" Another kick as I tried to crawl toward the door. "And then I'd give you those passwords, everything you asked me for, and I'd take the hit for it – huh? That was your bright plan, wasn't it? Well, you planned wrong, sweetheart."

He reached down and picked me up by the front of my jacket. His face, inches from mine, was mottled a furious red as my feet dangled above the floor.

"You said . . ." I struggled to get the words past my bloodied tongue. "Everything . . . would be all right . . ."

"Oh yeah. It'll be all right – for me." Pomeroy's sneer curled sharper. "Soon as I call up McIntyre and tell him what happened out here. Soon as I tell him what you tried to pull over on us. And when he sees what I've done to you – what I'm about to do – he'll know I was as mad about it as he'll be when I tell him."

"I can . . . get the money back . . ."

"Really?" Pomeroy's eyes narrowed as he peered at me. "That's not what Cole said."

All of a sudden, the room seemed bigger. As though the walls had fallen away, the roof peeling back to reveal the stars.

"Cole?" I could feel blood trickling down my chin as I raised my face toward the old man. "What . . . about him . . ."

"He's the one who called me," said Pomeroy. "We're old friends, the two of us. He did some good work down here once, for both me and McIntyre. I don't know how he found out about your little scheme, but I'm glad he did."

Ugly shapes were forming inside my head. With long, jagged shadows.

"This'll do him a lot of good, too." Pomeroy gave a slow nod, savoring what he saw in my eyes. "It's always good to do somebody like McIntyre a favor. Especially a big one like this. Maybe he'll find some kind of job for Cole, something he can do the way he is now. People like McIntyre can be really grateful."

"You're wrong . . . that's not . . . what happened . . ."

"Really? Think you can fool me twice?" His face darkened. "That pisses me off, sweetheart. Really pisses me off –"

He picked me up higher and threw me. My back hit the window, shattering the glass. I found myself on the sidewalk, surrounded by bright, glittering shards.

With his shoe, Pomeroy brushed away the daggers of glass sticking up from the window frame. Then he stepped over it, towering above me once again.

On the sidewalk, my hands left bloody prints, black in the moonlight. My raw fingertips caught the edge of the curb as I dragged myself toward it.

I felt Pomeroy grab my jacket collar. He pulled me up, then threw me forward again. I landed across the motorcycle, knocking it over onto its side.

"We got all night, Kim." I heard his voice somewhere above me. "There's more I'm going to do to you. A lot more . . ."

My fingers dug into the asphalt. Then they touched something softer.

The backpack.

I pulled it under myself and clawed at the zipper. When Pomeroy kicked me in the shoulder, rolling me over onto my back, I had the .357 in both hands.

I didn't have to remember anything that Cole had taught me. It just happened.

The first two shots caught Pomeroy in his chest, pushing him backward. He toppled, landing against the empty windowsill. He looked stunned, as I got to my feet and stood in front of him.

The rest of the shots echoed down the unlit street. When the gun was empty, I let it dangle at my side. Its weight drew me down to my knees. The old man's astonished gaze looked past me now, toward the moon.

TWENTY-TWO

AND THEN I rode some more.

Not back home, though I wanted to more than anything else. I just wanted to go there and let myself into that little space where the rest of the world wasn't. And just lie down on top of my brother's bed and wrap my arms around him. Just rock the two of us to sleep . . .

There wasn't going to be any sleep. I knew that. Not for a while, at least.

I'd left Pomeroy's body still lying on the sidewalk. Brushing bits of broken window glass from my jacket, I had slowly turned and listened. For police sirens, or any other indication that somebody had heard what had gone on. Nothing – in a broke small town like this, there was probably one police cruiser for the whole place. I knew I had at least a little time. Enough to go back inside and find a beat-up old first aid kit in the bathroom. It had the old kind of bandages, the ones with the skinny red thread you have to pull to tear open the sterile wrapper. I slapped a few on the worst cuts on my hands, then checked myself for any other damage. One side of my face was bruised and swollen from where the old man had hit me. That, plus my aching ribs and spine, seemed to be the extent of it.

I had been mainly worried about the motorcycle. If it wouldn't start up, then I was toast. I lifted it back upright and hit the ignition switch. There was a chug and a cough, plus the smell of spilled gasoline, and then the engine caught. I revved the throttle a couple of times to get it running smooth. I found my helmet and pulled it on, strapped the backpack with the emptied .357 to the seat, then climbed on and headed back to the city.

There was somebody waiting up for me, when I got to the warehouse. I could see a faint blue glow filling one of the skylights. I set the helmet down, unzipped the backpack, and took out the gun. This late, everything was so quiet that I could hear the waves lapping against the pilings of the wharves.

It wasn't Cole waiting. I made my way to the walled-off area and found his Monica sitting at the wobbly table, with the portable TV and the ashtray set on top of it. The TV's volume was turned down to a whisper as she sat watching with a cigarette in her hand.

She glanced over at me as I came in. "How'd things go?"

"What the hell do you care?" I figured she was in on it, on the whole mess that I had been set up for. There weren't a lot of secrets between her and Cole.

Carrying the gun, I walked over to the mattress. He was there, curled up under the blanket, asleep. The dim light carved shadows into the gaunt face laid on the pillow, his breath slow and ragged.

With the toe of my boot, I prodded the ammo boxes scattered around, until I found one that rattled with a few bullets left inside it. I shook them out into the palm of my hand, opened the .357 and loaded it up. Then I turned back to where Cole lay.

I pointed the barrel straight down at his head.

Monica coolly watched me. "Sure that's what you want to do?"

"I don't know." I kept my finger on the curve of the trigger. "I don't know anything. I never did."

"But now you do."

I looked over at her. "Like what?"

"Who you are."

What that was supposed to mean, I had no idea.

"I'm the same as I was before," I said. "Except screwed over a little more."

"That counts." She flicked ash from the cigarette. "But now you know what that is. You wouldn't know, if it weren't for him."

"What makes you think I wanted to know?"

She didn't have a smart answer for that.

"Besides," I said. "He set me up. I could've been dead by now."

"But you're not." Monica smiled. "Now I owe him five bucks. I wasn't sure you'd pull it off. But he thought you would. Looks like he was right."

"I'm not following you." The gun's weight was starting to tremble in my outstretched hand. That's how exhausted I was. "Right about what?"

"Taking care of that old man. That's why Cole phoned him and told him what was going on. Some of it, at least. So the old man would be ready for you. And pissed off. Then you'd have to take care of him. You'd have to be what you really are." Another drag from the cigarette, then the smile again. "Whether you like it or not."

"Crap." My brain felt tired. It'd been a long night. All I'd wanted to do was come back here and blow a hole through Cole's head. And now I was caught up in another one of these weird discussions. "So why? Why'd he want to do that?"

"Because you've got work to do. The two of you. And you gotta be ready for it. That's all."

I started to see what she was talking about. Probably not a good sign.

"Ready," I said. "Okay . . ."

"Think about it." Monica seemed pleased with her explanation. "Going after McIntyre isn't going to be easy. The two of you are likely to wind up in a pretty tight place. That's not going to be the time to find out what you really are. Now you both know. Now you can get to work."

She was right, I knew. Now we could. Cole and me.

"But if you want to . . ." She nodded toward the gun in my hand. "Go ahead. It's not like I'm going to stop you. Maybe it'd be better that way."

My finger loosened from the trigger. I couldn't do it; I knew that as well. I didn't hate him enough. Or at least not yet.

I lowered the gun, from where it had been pointing straight at the side of Cole's head.

"Why couldn't he just tell me." I didn't even know who I was talking to, Monica or just myself. "That's all he would've had to do."

"That's not how it works," said Monica quietly. "Not in this world."

The gun dangled useless in my hand. I was done for the night.

"You'll have to excuse Cole for not waking up and telling you all this himself." She stubbed out the cigarette butt in the ashtray. "He's on some pain medications that really knock him out. He doesn't take them when he's working with you."

I didn't say anything. I just turned and walked out of the warehouse, carrying the gun with me.

† † †

On the ride home, I got that weird sensation again.

The streets slowly rolled by. All the city buildings, wrapped in night, flattened insubstantial. Fakes, none of them real, painted on overlaid transparencies. I felt like I could pull the motorcycle over and climb off it, then push my hand right through everything I saw. As tired as I was, that still scared me a little.

I let myself into the apartment and threw my helmet and the backpack, heavy again with the gun, onto the couch. Feeling a million years old, I walked back to the bedroom.

Donnie was waiting up for me. I knew he would be.

"You're really late." He watched me as I sat down next to him on the bed. "You okay?"

"Sure," I said. "Maybe."

I knew I wasn't. I was all messed up. Everything in the bedroom was flat and two-dimensional. I was afraid that its edges would curl upward, and the things I had just barely glimpsed before, with their cold dead gaze, would peer out at me. Watching and waiting.

With my eyes squeezed shut, I wrapped my arms around him. I was afraid to let go. I was afraid to open my eyes. What if I did, and he wasn't there, either? Not really there. Then where would I be?

"Kimmie . . ."

For a moment longer, I couldn't. Then I opened my eyes and looked.

And he was there. For real. Still.

"Are you going to be all right?" He sounded worried.

It took another moment for me to answer. Then I nodded.

"Yeah, I think so." I let go of him a little, so we both could breathe. "We'll both be okay. I'm working on it."

He laid back down on the pillow and looked up at me. "You need to get some sleep."

"You're right," I said. I gave him a smile. "I got a job to do."

12702181R00114

Printed in Great Britain
by Amazon.co.uk, Ltd.,
Marston Gate.